BELOW THE BELT

A dizzying blow to the side of Ki's face sent him reeling. Another to his ribs doubled him over where he lay. Ki sat up as Bartlett heaved a sidearm blow. In one move, Ki ducked his head and landed a devastating upward thrust with the heel of his hand into Bartlett's crotch. Bartlett hit the floor, clutching his abdomen in speechless agony, turning pale, eyes rolling backward, and falling into a dead faint . . .

DON'T MISS THESE
ALL-ACTION WESTERN SERIES
FROM THE BERKLEY PUBLISHING GROUP

THE GUNSMITH by J. R. Roberts
>Clint Adams was a legend among lawmen, outlaws, and ladies. They called him . . . the Gunsmith.

LONGARM by Tabor Evans
>The popular long-running series about U.S. Deputy Marshal Long—his life, his loves, his fight for justice.

LONE STAR by Wesley Ellis
>The blazing adventures of Jessica Starbuck and the martial arts master, Ki. Over eight million copies in print.

SLOCUM by Jake Logan
>Today's longest-running action Western. John Slocum rides a deadly trail of hot blood and cold steel.

WESLEY ELLIS

LONE STAR

IN THE SIERRA DIABLOS

JOVE BOOKS, NEW YORK

LONE STAR IN THE SIERRA DIABLOS

A Jove Book / published by arrangement with
the author

PRINTING HISTORY
Jove edition / August 1994

ISBN: 0-515-11436-7

A JOVE BOOK®
Jove Books are published by The Berkley Publishing Group,
200 Madison Avenue, New York, New York 10016.
JOVE and the "J" design are trademarks
belonging to Jove Publications, Inc.

PRINTED IN THE UNITED STATES OF AMERICA

10 9 8 7 6 5 4 3 2 1

★

Chapter 1

A killing frost was about to seize West Texas in its brittle grip. Jessie could feel it coming. By dawn, icy needles over most every surface in her room at Pritchard's Inn made her clamp her eyes shut, pull the quilts high over her head, and snuggle in deep. She wanted to stay there until the weather remembered that this was Sarah, Texas, where it wasn't supposed to get so cold.

It wasn't until after ten o'clock that she finally rose, pulling a comforter around her shoulders, and got Widow Pritchard to bring some heated water. The long sleep had done Jessie a heap of good, bone-weary as she was after her long trip from Austin. Feeling rested and game, she combed her long copper-blond hair and let it cascade over her voluptuous, full breasts. She shook out her Levi's and chose a fresh silk shirt. She dressed, all but for her boots.

The late winter sunlight drew her to the rear door leading out onto a second-story porch. The moment the door came unstuck with a creak it was apparent that it was warmer outside than it was in the room, though she could still see her breath in the fresh morning air. A deep blue sky, as clear today as it was leaden the day before, lifted her spirits. The dirt courtyard below, bordered by the back sides of several buildings and the livery stable, was empty and quiet except for the sparrows in the cottonwoods at the far side. Jessie stepped onto the porch and leaned over the rail to inhale in the sunlight. She stretched and yawned. She turned away and stooped for her boots, knocking them together to loosen the caked mud.

From the courtyard below came a woman's voice, calling, "Señor Vargas! Antonio Vargas!"

Jessie glanced over her shoulder and saw a young woman in a dark woolen dress walking out from under the cottonwoods, her hands, inside a furry muff, protected from the chill. Even at a distance her smile was attractive. Two well-dressed men paused from hitching their horses to a rail close by the porch of the inn. They had the look of successful ranchers.

"Good morning, sir," the woman continued, her voice becoming lower as she approached. "You're looking very well today."

Jessie turned away again to scrape the stubborn clods, taking little notice that one of the men, a robust white-haired gentleman, had removed his hat and was smiling as he stepped out to meet the pretty lady. He extended his right hand. Jessie knocked the boots together twice more, feeling the pleasant stretch in her thighs. She picked up a bridle, and stood up.

Two gunshots rang out, close together. Flat pops with no echo. Jessie hit the floor, then peeked over the edge of the porch on all fours. There in the yard stood the young woman still pointing her pistol at the old man, fallen at her feet. His right leg was bent at an unnatural angle beneath him. The second man, yelling, "Murder!" and calling for help, took cover behind his horse. Dust raised by his feet followed the gun smoke. Wisps of dust across the yard made a slow retreat upon the cold breeze. To Jessie's amazement the woman calmly squeezed two more shots into her victim, one to the gut, one to the head. Instantly he fell still, his left hand looming clawlike above his reddening chest. Without hurry she proceeded to walk back the way she came, emptying the chambers of the gun into her palm as she went.

Crouching behind the porch rail, Jessie stifled a yell as the dark-haired second man ran forward and fell beside the dead man and held the slack-jawed face. His eyes darted. He reached out and lifted a small pistol from the dead man's right hand and stuffed it into his own vest. "Murderer!" he shouted. "Murderer!" Townspeople seeped out of doorways and alleys and poured into the yard. "Stop her!" But no one did, not until the woman dropped her pistol to the ground. Men crept forward, unsure what to do. Someone raised a hand to halt her while keeping his other on his holster. In a few moments a tall, ponytailed man in a long black overcoat trotted into the clearing. On his breast a silver star glinted in the sunlight. He lingered for a look at the dead man. Stooping, he held open the man's coat and ran one hand down each side of his body. He patted the trousers down to the ankles and felt along the belt line, front and back. Straightening his coat, the lawman shouldered his way through the gathering crowd toward the shooter. Jessie descended the staircase as soon as her boots were on. Nearing the crowd, she heard someone call her name. It was Ki.

"What happened?"

"Man's been shot," Jessie replied, "but I doubt that's all. Ki, do you know if Marshal Haskins has deputized anyone recently?"

"No."

Ki stayed close to her as she melted through the onlookers. Besides being her closest lifetime friend, he was her bodyguard, a duty he took more seriously than any other. Half Japanese, half Caucasian, Ki could almost pass as a full-blooded American until one got a closer look at his almond eyes. Standing a bit more than six feet tall, he was an impressive sight, from his jet-black ponytailed hair to his lean, muscular legs and cork-soled slippers. He discreetly observed the entire crowd, barely letting Jessie out of his sight.

There was movement everywhere. Shouts went up for Dr. MacNaughton, and a man ran off to fetch him. He was followed by several excited young boys. The ponytailed lawman searched the crowd and directed two men to guard the woman while he inspected the body. All the while the dead man's escort harangued him and the killer, pointing into his own face to emphasize that he had seen it with his own two eyes.

"Who's the deadliner?" asked Ki.

"That's old man Vargas," Jessie said quietly, "so I guess the other guy must be his son, Wilfredo."

"And the woman?"

Jessie shook her head. "Never saw her before."

The crowd grew denser. The deputy told people to stand back, and when that proved futile, he instructed two men to remove the suspect to Whittaker's Dry Goods. This drew a loud reaction from Wilfredo Vargas, who continued to hurl invectives. The lawman tried to get him to retell the incident calmly. Vargas cried, "*Mira*. She murder my father in cold blood." He recounted his father's movements with increasingly wild gestures, summarizing with loud repetitions of "She murder my father!" He spit on the ground and growled, "She must pay! Yes? She *will* pay for what she do to my father!"

Dr. MacNaughton arrived with his adolescent entourage. He scowled at the sight of the dead man and pulled at his snowy beard. He knelt beside him. It didn't take a doctor to tell old man Vargas was no more. If the neat black and red hole just above his half-closed eyes weren't enough to tell, surely the ragged exit wound at the back of his head was. The doctor counted three wounds, stood erect, and before going off to prepare a death certificate told the lawman he'd be available.

It was all the marshal could do to keep things manageable as he strutted off to Whittaker's store to arrest

4

the young woman. Vargas stayed close behind, repeating for all to hear that the killing had been in cold blood. That was Jessie's cue to follow.

At the door to Whittaker's the tall lawman turned to prevent anyone else from entering. Jessie was practically thrust into his chest by the pressing crowd. She read the word "Deputy" on his badge.

"Clear the way, folks; there's nothing more to see," he said, trying to edge into the door.

Jessie touched his arm. "Deputy, I am Jessica Starbuck."

He looked hard at her and Ki with no sign of recognition. *Obviously a newcomer to Sarah*, Ki thought.

She stated, "I saw what happened. I was up there on that porch."

Vargas' eyes seemed to drill holes into her face. His deep-hued face was moist. The deputy gave them both a quick glance and, guiding her inside with a hand on her shoulder, said, "C'mon in—and nobody else! Mr. Vargas, please wait outside until I ask for you."

In a chair before the counter, surrounded by kegs of nails and bales of wire, sat the shooter. Calm, collected, confident, she looked up when they entered. With her hands tucked within her muff she sat erect, dignified. Her clothing was neat and apparently expensive. Long chestnut hair was plaited and neatly wrapped in a bun. Her smooth complexion was flush and the slightest hint of a smile lifted her high, round cheekbones beneath strong eyes. She was gorgeous.

One of the men handed the lawman a pistol and three cartridges, indicating with a nod that they belonged to the lady. While another man stood guard Mr. Whittaker stoked the wood stove. Faces crowded the small-paned windows as onlookers peered in for a glimpse of the harmless-looking, yet already notorious, murderess. Ignoring them entirely, she remained unperturbed.

"Good morning, Marshal," she said.

With a drawl that marked him as being from east of the Ozarks, the lawman corrected her. "Deputy marshal, ma'am, duly appointed. Name's Boyd Barefoot."

5

She responded without hesitation, "I am Leslie Sykes," striking a spark of recognition in Jessie's mind. The family name was familiar.

Deputy Barefoot settled himself atop a barrel, never taking his eyes from the woman. "Tell me about yourself, Miss Sykes."

"I killed Antonio Vargas—in a fair fight, of course. Although I would have killed him anyway." Her brow rose in a slender arch. "Isn't that what you need to know, Marshal Barefeet?"

Mr. Whittaker stepped closer and inclined his head as if he hadn't heard correctly. He pulled on his thick walrus mustache. Her bluntness surprised everyone.

"That's 'Barefoot,' ma'am, and I'm only a deputy. Duly appointed. Anything else to tell me?" asked Barefoot.

"He killed my father after robbing us of everything that mattered: our home, our cattle, the very land we have lived on and legally owned for over a hundred years."

Jessie's heart fluttered. The woman before her was none other than the daughter of Emmet Sykes, whose murder eighteen months ago, while officially unsolved, reputedly involved the Vargas family and was a hot topic of gossip throughout West Texas at the time.

Emmet Sykes and four generations of Sykeses before him had owned a respectable tract of grazing land and chaparral—a mere seven thousand acres, give or take a fence post—in the hills west of Sarah and the Circle Star holdings. Most of the land had stood as open range, as it had for centuries before the Spanish crown granted it, and more, to a prominent hacendado named Don Enrique de Málaga. It was from him that Great-granddad Sykes ultimately bought his acreage.

Then, just two years ago, came Antonio Vargas, whose family roots went deeper into the soil of West Texas and Sonora than any Lone Star loyalist alive. He presented himself to state and federal authorities bearing a deed that assigned to one Paolo Málaga, heir to the original grantee, a twelve-hundred-square-mile

6

tract, more than three quarters of a million acres. The deed was dated 1773—two years before Great-granddad Sykes supposedly bought his parcel from Don Enrique. It was through Paolo that the land passed into the Vargas family. Not only was Vargas's deed older than Sykes's but also there was a 107-year-old paper trail of tenant agreements, surveys, purchases, sales, and bequeathals that provided indisputable additional proof that the Sykes—and dozens of other ranchers, farmers, miners, railway companies, and engineers— were mere trespassers—unless they paid to stay.

Rumor had it Emmet Sykes hated taxes. That was because he was the type that could never see his way clear to paying more for something he was damn sure was already his, and he was certain he owned the land of his ancestors. Meanwhile, most folks, if asked, would tell you only fools fooled with Vargas. Emmet Sykes was no fool, but he found out the hard way what that tale meant to folks in those parts. So young Leslie Sykes fooled with old Vargas as no one ever had before or ever would again. There she sat, cool like slate in December, and apparently no fool.

Jessie hadn't known that Emmet Sykes even had a daughter. And if Jessie hadn't know, chances were no one in Sarah had, particularly the deputy. He was new to everything here, Jessie judged. He continued to address the men helping him as Mr. Adams and Mr. Judd, instead of simple Brant or Howie, as every one knew them; but he handled himself well, speaking evenly, asking all the right questions, apparently memorizing everything Leslie said. Barefoot was no tenderfoot.

He prompted her. "You say you killed Mr. Vargas in self-defense."

"No, sir," Leslie answered. "In a fair fight. I wasn't so much defending myself as avenging my father."

"Are you confessing to the murder of Antonio Vargas?" he asked.

"No. It was not murder."

"What was it, then?"

7

"As I said, Deputy: a fair fight."

Barefoot winced. "With an unarmed man?"

"He was not unarmed," was Sykes's reply. "No Vargas is ever unarmed."

"Well that goes for about ev'ry Texan standing, miss," said Barefoot, "but there just weren't no weapon on him this fine mornin'."

Miss Sykes forced an exhale. "Doesn't surprise me," she said, shaking her head.

"What doesn't, Miss Sykes?"

The pretty, dark-eyed woman stared up at Barefoot with her intriguing dimpled smile and slowly replied, "Nothing. None of this."

"Care to explain?"

She huffed. "Either you just didn't look well enough for a weapon, sir, or you're on the Vargas payroll, too."

The tall deputy politely told her that he had checked the body thoroughly—it was one of the first things a lawman did when gun smoke had a chance to clear—and no gun was found. With apologies he informed her that he would have to arrest her for murder and hold her in a jail cell, unbefitting a lady. He instructed Adams and Judd to see to her, and when they had gone out the front door, he turned to Jessie.

"Sorry to disfurnish you, Miss Starbuck." He extended his hand. "It's a pleasure meeting you. I heard you been trav'ling."

Jessie was taken aback. Suddenly he seemed to know all about her, and he even managed a smile. His large hand was warm, his grip like a firm embrace. Mention of her business trip reminded her of some valuables left in her room and made her uneasy. When Jessie found words, she admitted to being at a loss. Before she left for Austin, Marshal Haskins had been passing the days quietly on a chair outside Bennett's Tonsorial Parlor, swapping tall tales with the owner. Today Sarah had a new deputy marshal she had never met before, and there was murder in the street.

She asked the deputy's indulgence by allowing her to get a message to Ki. Barefoot opened the door for her and beckoned Jessie's friend inside. As they introduced themselves to each other Jessie smiled at the sight of the two ponytailed men. She briefly instructed Ki to remain in her room until she could return, indicating that her saddlebags were beneath the bed.

The contents of those bags were of no small concern. Ever since Jessie had assumed full control over all the Starbuck enterprises upon the untimely death of her father, Alex Starbuck, she'd had to hold together some of the most far-flung, most influential business operations America's private sector had yet seen. After the depression and the international scandals of the early 1870s, and the fitful postwar reconstruction, the economy was now booming. And the Starbuck empire was as much behind the boom as it was a part of it.

Alex Starbuck was an extraordinary man. Larger than life. More than just founder of the town of Sarah, he was a man respected by presidents, consulted by senators, and hated by usurpers of American free enterprise. His vision took shape first through the import-export business that brought the riches of Asia to American shores and found Alex the Japanese housekeeper who would become mentor to young Jessie. Later his business in Japan brought to him the powerful young warrior who, because his blood was tainted by that of the "barbarian" Caucasian, was rejected by his own people. This warrior called himself only Ki, derived from *kiai* the Japanese word for "spirit yell," and he traveled to America, where he again found himself outcast. There he dedicated himself to the service of his only true benefactor, Alex Starbuck, by assuming the duties of bodyguard, teacher, and friend to Alex's only daughter, Jessica.

The timing was ideal. For Alex also waged an unending war against a lawless international cabal intent upon illegally seizing control of America, all its riches and assets. Alex fought them in every arena of business, every chamber of politics, and on every bloody field of honor until the day he himself fell at the hands of assassins. For Jessie the loss was total, due not only to the boundless love she had for him but also to the similar fate that befell her mother, namesake of the town of Sarah, when Jessie was still a girl.

All that Jessie had, all that Jessie was, came from them, and especially from her father. He was determined to make his gutsy young girl equal to or better than anyone, man or woman. He taught her how to ride and how to shoot, how to converse and how to negotiate, how to do good business and how to distinguish between right and wrong. Perhaps most of all he taught her about the cabal and even left an encoded notebook listing all their known agents, who were crippling America from within. What he could not teach her—when, where, and how they would show themselves, and how to fight them—Jessie had to learn on her own.

Cattle comprised the core of Starbuck operations at the Circle Star Ranch. Of course, Jessie oversaw the myriad other Starbuck enterprises and conducted all related business. Thus, the safety of her unattended saddlebags concerned her.

While at the capital to address concerns of the local cattlemen's association Jessie also finalized an investment in the work of an old friend of her father, an inventor. Through her broker she purchased bearer bonds to raise capital for this inventor's new meat-packing process, an advance he hoped might someday revolutionize the operations of Armour, Swift, and Hormel. Though the bonds were only as safe as cash, not being registered, they were a small ante for a winning hand. Basically legal tender and payable to the bearer, whoever that may be, the bonds demanded to be guarded at all times, and Jessie, in the excitement following the shooting, had forgotten them. She felt very much relieved knowing that Ki had found the saddlebags still beneath her bed, unmolested— all $10,000 worth. An incredible fortune some would kill for.

Barefoot stared long into Jessie's wide green eyes. He had heard how beautiful she was, but facing her now, he found her almost unbelievable. Her broken-in denims hugged her plump bottom and shapely thighs the way he only wished he could hug her himself. Her square brass belt buckle rested against a flat tummy draped with a white silk blouse that spoke of excellent taste and the ability to afford it. Even the weak winter sun hadn't allowed her skin to lose its bronze. Jessie folded her arms across her chest and shivered.

From across the room Whittaker called out, "Git her on over to the stove, y'dang fool! Can't ya see she's turnin' blue?" As he prepared a seat for her close by, he moaned, "Dern young'uns these days don't know manners from mule turd. Whole dang country's goin' down." Jessie tried to conceal her smile as she extended her palms over the stove, and Barefoot falteringly spoke.

"Well, ma'am—"

"Call me Jessie. Please."

"Well, Miss Jessie, you heard what Miss Sykes had to say. Anything you might add? Change?"

She rubbed her hands together.

"Antonio Vargas definitely had a gun."

"Shoot! I searched him myself," Barefoot countered. "Weren't nothing on him."

"I saw Wilfredo Vargas take a small pistol from his father's right hand. He stashed it in his coat before anyone saw him."

"You sure?"

"Sure as I'm sitting here now. You find that gun right away and you'll probably also find one chamber spent. I heard four shots altogether; there were two before I saw Miss Sykes fire two more."

"Miss Jessie, are you willing to testify to that in a court of law?"

She swallowed. "Whatever's necessary, Deputy."

"Please, ma'am, call me Boyd." He crossed the cluttered room and rubbed his chin. "You know, Miss Jessie—and you may not care to hear this, but—

11

besides Vargas, you're the only real witness in this damn case."

"Some witness," Jessie replied dejectedly. "I can't even tell who fired first!"

★
Chapter 2

When Deputy Barefoot asked Jessie to remain in town until the course of the case became clearer, one part of her wanted to refuse. It seemed within her rights. She was only hours away from home—from the great gray slate fireplace in the expansive room where there hung the portrait of Jessie's mother, the study that was the heart of Starbuck business since her father's days, still redolent with the cherry aroma of his pipe tobacco. She yearned to be in that room and imagined she was, with its gleaming glass-windowed gun cabinets, fine leather furniture, and huge old desk of scarred oak, which her father had owned since his first days in San Francisco. Instead, here she was, in Sarah. She agreed to remain in town because it was the responsible thing to do. There were always Starbuck employees passing through, so she'd be in contact and it made her feel safe, and there were things she wanted to do before leaving.

Most of all, she wanted to find out whether this lone Sykes woman could be hatching a scheme to save

13

herself or was just plain willing to forfeit her own life as the price of vengeance. Or perhaps she had been grazing on locoweed. Then there was Boyd Barefoot, a new face in town, and an attractive one at that. Though she didn't admit to it aloud, even Ki could tell that Jessie's curiosity about the new deputy went beyond his professional credentials.

So it wasn't entirely reluctantly that when two ranch hands and the cook from the Circle Star rolled into Sarah for supplies the next day, Jessie decided to send them back with the message that her return would be delayed until further notice.

So instead of taking her on as a passenger and heading home directly, they spent much of the day apprising her of the ranch's status during her absence. They all took a meal at Boney's Saloon, where the beer mugs were large, the chili could kill a cat, and the conversation at every table hovered around the killing of Antonio Vargas. By midafternoon, their buckboard was fully loaded, and the three men started back for the Circle Star without Jessie. The town of Sarah being practically Jessie's own home turf, she held no suspicion toward most people there, stranger or native. So it was natural for her to miss the two swarthy men at the table next to hers who left Boney's just before she and her boys did, two men who seemed more interested in what Jessie had to say than in the beans and corn bread they were washing down with giggle-soup.

As the wagon rolled out of sight on its way back to the ranch a chill wind passed through Jessie's fleece-lined coat. Made her shiver. With a shrug she pulled her collar closed, turned on her heels to go, and slammed face first into the midnight expanse of black fabric across Deputy Barefoot's broad chest. With a reflexive yelp she bounced back, frightened, as Barefoot grunted and threw his arms up uselessly to absorb the shock. His apologies became urgent when he noticed how badly she had hurt her nose. Jessie was too busy checking for blood to be embarrassed. She felt dizzy. Barefoot led her to a chair outside Boney's, apologizing the entire time. Finally Jessie said, "Please stop saying you're sorry. It was my fault." And he stopped.

Gently pulling her hands from her face, he said, "Here, let's see," and reassured her that her nose was as beautiful as ever.

"I guess that means we've officially met," Jessie said.

"We can almost say we know each other," said Barefoot. The weight he placed on the word "know" elicited a sly glance from the blushing young woman.

"Not quite yet," she said, then smiled. "Although the idea did cross my mind."

Barefoot's eyes lowered a moment. His ears reddened.

"I was coming to tell you that Wilfredo Vargas plans to press his own charges against Miss Sykes if she ain't indicted. Either which way, you're swimming in the stew pot."

Jessie shrugged. Sniffling, she squeezed the bridge of her nose.

"I been there before, Deputy. Nothing new." She stood up and announced, "I was just headed back to my room. Care to walk?"

A gust of icy wind hit them from behind, causing their clothing to flap and wisps of dust to skim down the unpaved street. With her hands thrust deep into her pockets Jessie broached the subject of Marshal Haskins with new deputy.

There was little mystery to it. After years of wearing a badge, from his home in Memphis to the mining camps of the San Juans, Barefoot had found himself driving cattle along the Ellsworth and other trails. The rail head at Council Grove, Kansas, was one such place he came to know well, especially one autumn because of a well-organized rustling scam. That was where Barefoot suddenly found himself volunteered for a posse by a brassy young deputy named Isaiah Haskins. The ambushes and shoot-outs that ensued over the following several days didn't turn out the way Law and Order would have it, but Haskins' life had been saved by Barefoot in a showdown that defied logic and challenged belief. Although Barefoot denied having any amount of Indian blood in him, Haskins always said it must have been "strong Injun medicine" that kept the lead from Barefoot's flesh that day. That was nearly eight years ago. And Haskins never forgot it.

A day or two after Jessie left for Austin, Barefoot had ridden into Sarah, and the two lawmen were briefly reacquainted. But as marshal, Haskins, too, was on the move, having been called out to quell a minor feud a few days north of town, with barely enough time to appoint a deputy for the interim. They determined to catch up on the old days when Haskins returned.

"So here I am," Barefoot concluded, "deputy marshal and acting head of the Committee for Public Safety of Sarah."

Jessie laughed out loud. "Of course! I should have guessed."

Barefoot later asked Jessie to clarify some pieces of the deposition she had given him the day before, regarding what she saw in the courtyard. The question whether old man Vargas did, in fact, have a weapon in his right hand gnawed at him. Barefoot had also searched his son, Wilfredo, immediately after Jessie had suggested he had taken the pistol, but Wilfredo wasn't packing. They both realized that the younger Vargas would have had plenty of time to pass the gun off to someone or hide it. Jessie admitted she thought Vargas was just inviting Miss Sykes to shake hands at first. His right hand didn't look suspicious from where Jessie was, but she couldn't see his palm. Yet she was certain of what she saw Wilfredo do.

"I distinctly saw him place both hands on his father's cheeks, like this, as if he was going to shake him some," she affirmed, with her palms facing each other before her. "He definitely took something from his father's right hand, and it sure looked like a gun to me, a mighty small one."

Barefoot told her that her account of hearing four shots didn't mesh with Wilfredo's account of three, all of them fired at his father. Jessie went silent, perturbed by self-doubt. Was there a chance she was wrong? She clearly recalled seeing two puffs of gun smoke drift past Miss Sykes before the final two shots were fired.

As they walked, Jessie noticed a small boy crossing the road ahead. As another cold gust of wind snuck up from behind, the boy kicked a stone and raised a veil of dust at his feet. Another several yards off, a puff of dust lifted into the wind where the stone touched ground. The cottonwoods on the far side of the courtyard flashed through her mind.

"He did fire!" she announced emphatically. "Vargas definitely fired that gun! Boyd, I saw *two* clouds of smoke from the guns. But there was also a puff of dust, like by the trees a way behind Leslie Sykes. I just thought it was the wind churning things up some! It didn't occur to me before: that's where Vargas' bullet must have struck the tree. I'd bet on it!"

In moments they were standing before the cottonwoods, staring closely at the thick corrugated bark of one tree, then another. Finding nothing, Barefoot sighed and stood with his arms akimbo, thinking. He turned and walked to where Vargas had fallen, then turned again to face the trees. He asked Jessie to stand where she thought Miss Sykes was standing when she pulled the trigger. By now, several townsfolk were standing at the edge of the courtyard watching their little reenactment. A short, dark-skinned man stepped forward from between two buildings and stared.

Barefoot guessed, "Vargas ended on his back; so if this is where he fell, he was probably one or two steps forward when he took the first bullet—about here like." He raised his right hand. "Now, if he had the gun thuswise, and she was drawing her gun with her right hand, how'd he miss her and hit a tree?"

"I know what I'd do," Jessie said. Pretending to have her hands buried in a muff, she drew her hand, first finger extended, while deflecting Barefoot's gun hand with her left forearm. "I'd do the quickest little dance

17

you ever didn't see, like this. You'd miss if I was quick enough," she said.

"You'd have to be mighty fast, or leastways I'd graze you bad."

"And if you didn't graze me?"

He looked beyond her shoulder and said, "I'd prob'ly bury some lead in that tree right there." He quickly stepped forward. As if he had seen the incident in a psychic vision, he walked directly to one tree in particular, looked it over with his hands, and shouted back to Jessie, "Found it!"

Antonio Vargas' stray shot had flicked off a silver-dollar-sized piece of bark and drilled a shallow hole into the tree. Barefoot worked at it with his folding knife and, with a look of pleased surprise, held out his palm for Jessie to see a badly mashed piece of lead, probably .32 caliber, he guessed.

As the onlookers whispered among themselves no one noticed that the short, dark-skinned man was no longer among them.

The next day dawned icy and clear, but by midday a changing sky and shifting wind foretold bitter weather. Inside Boney's saloon, however, the large oil furnace, its florid embossing blackened by use, kept the room as warm as a Texas summer. Jessie and Ki sat at a table close to it, relaxing after a lazy afternoon meal. Their conversation was suddenly interrupted by a cold draft when the front door was noisily thrown wide.

"Miss Starbuck,"—it was Howie Judd, looking agitated—"come quick!"

On the street people stood aghast at the sight of two men leading their horses toward the jail house. Lashed across the animals' backs were the limp bodies of three men, their hair whitened by the dusty West Texas wind, their clothing blotched by patches of dried blood. Down the street Deputy Barefoot stepped out of his office, having also been summoned to witness the grisly sight. A chill overtook Jessie as she recognized the three corpses as the Circle Star men who had left town the day before. She and Ki hurried alongside the horses toward the San Pedro Infirmary, where Barefoot came out to meet them.

Horror showed in Jessie's eyes as the bodies were lifted down and brought inside. Barefoot helped, barely able to disguise his own revulsion. The two travelers who brought them in, cowhands Jessie knew from a neighboring ranch, gave their account with tremors in their voices.

They had found them a few miles from where they picked up the road into Sarah. They recognized them as Circle Star men right off. The Circle Star wagon lay toppled in a gully, but the supplies it had carried were strewn a long way down the road, on both sides. It was several hundred yards farther where the bodies lay, two of them near each other, the third far off the road, facedown. Their rifles lay where they fell.

After a quick inspection Barefoot pulled a small leather pouch from inside one man's shirt and sighed, "Well, it weren't no robbery, I'd venture." He emptied the pouch into his palm, showing several dollars in half eagles and change. "Ain't no road agent what's gonna leave this behind."

"These men was bushwhacked by rimrockers, Marshal," said one cowpoke. He looked hard at Barefoot through watery eyes that floated above a thin tangle of beard.

Barefoot seemed puzzled for a moment, then replied, "That's *deputy* marshal. Duly appointed."

"Duly or not, these men didn't see it comin'. Looky here—" He pointed to one of the unfortunates. "Throat's cut clear to the bone. Sidewinder did this had to get right smart close to a armed man for to do that."

His partner chimed in, pointing to another victim. "And that'un thar's been back-shot. Found him off the road a piece. Reckon them yeller bellies ran him down. Hell, looks to me like them damn Apaches gittin' brazen agin."

Voices rose in argument, and Barefoot waved his hand to calm things down. Ki looked Jessie in the

19

eye and discreetly shook his head. Jessie correctly interpreted that to mean he neither believed Apaches were the culprits nor thought it was a coincidence. She breathed deeply with trepidation and decided to have a word with Barefoot afterward.

Dr. MacNaughton entered, appearing glum. He cursed beneath his breath in his crooked Scots accent and proceeded to inspect the bodies. "So this is the reputation our town earns for itself, aye? Brilliant!" he complained. "Folks can't seem to carry on without killing each other like bleedin' savages."

Jessie and Ki waited for Barefoot outside. Dandridge, who ran a photography studio on the other side of town, came running toward the infirmary with an assistant. They hefted his enormous black camera and an unwieldly crate of glass negatives and supplies, prepared to immortalize the slain ranch hands before they were carted off to the deadline. Barefoot came out to the boardwalk, scuffing his heels.

"Boyd, I'd like to have a few words with Leslie Sykes," Jessie said.

The deputy frowned. "I plumb ain't sure that's the thing to do, Miss Jessie, you being an impartial witness and all. Don't think a judge would look kindly on that sort o'thing. Might make him mad as fire. But Vargas' attorney sure wouldn't mind none."

"May I see her?" asked Ki. "I'm not a witness."

"No," agreed Barefoot, "and you ain't impartial neither." He thought a while longer, glanced into Jessie's enticing green eyes. In a moment he was falling helplessly into their warmth. He turned to Ki. "I'll trust you not to do nothing that wouldn't be proper and legal."

"You can trust me," said Ki.

A small, sturdy brick building, the jail house was dimly lit by two oil lamps, far apart. The room was warm and filled with odor of the wood stove in the center, glowing beneath the low ceiling and raw timber rafters. The four cells were located through a rear door made of iron bars. They, too, were well heated, by an oil furnace which didn't need constant tending. Leslie Sykes was the deputy's only guest, the quiet town of Sarah seldom playing host to the types of tenants who frequent such quarters. Made of heavy strap iron riveted together vertically and horizontally, the cells were not uncomfortably small, and Miss Sykes enjoyed a certain amount of privacy, her cell being tucked into a corner and having a curtain raised on two sides by her host. When Deputy Barefoot allowed Ki to enter, the curtain was already pulled open on the front side. Beside the bed stood a table bearing a lamp and some papers. A wooden armchair—the marshal's, Ki knew— had a pillow on its seat. Leslie Sykes stood inside with her head down and her back to the door, as if unaware of—or simply disinterested in—the sound of the heavy iron door unlocking.

"Hello, Miss Sykes," Ki said.

She turned, holding an open book, and as their eyes met, Ki tried to ignore the flare of excitement which the sight of so beautiful a woman sparked inside him. Her eyes widened and her brows rose. Her high cheekbones became brighter with color. She stared into Ki's feral eyes for what seemed like minutes but otherwise stood stock-still.

"I am Ki. May I speak with you?"

She smiled softly. "Well, you don't appear to be the marshal, and I hope you're not a minister. You're far too handsome." Her smile widened. "I don't suppose, with hair like yours, that you and Marshal Barefeet could be related?"

Ki looked at the deputy, waiting by the door. Barefoot took Leslie's tease with a smile.

The implacable woman said more loudly, "Perhaps the duly appointed deputy would be courteous enough to allow my guest in!"

As Barefoot opened the cell door he asked, "Would the lady care for anything to eat or drink? Tea? Crumpets? Champagne?"

"Yes," she replied, "a glass of Amontillado at the Tremont Hotel in Galveston."

Barefoot looked at Ki as if to say, *She's all yours, pard,* and let him in. The exchange had an air of familiarity. She placed her book down on the table and invited Ki to sit, then waited for him to initiate the conversation. He noticed the title of her book: *Das Kapital,* by Karl Marx.

"Interesting reading?" he began self-consciously.

Ki couldn't tell if she looked disappointed with his poor opening or if she was considering an involved reply. She shrugged and said, "I'm really just practicing my French. I really don't understand it all."

"Are you a Marxist?"

She laughed. "No. Even Karl Marx is not a Marxist. He has some truth to tell, but he's a naive idealist. I prefer my revolutionaries to have firsthand experience before they begin preaching revolution."

"Does a person have to take a gun in hand to know what needs changing?" Ki said. "Maybe knowing what people need is enough."

"Marx somehow doesn't know people—the strong and the weak—or the nature of power and desire. Do you know the difference, Ki?"

"Desire allows one to dream," he said. "Power allows one to do."

"The two together can be magnificent," she said. She smiled her delicious smile again. "I don't dream, Ki. *I do.*"

"I see that," he responded, "judging from your actions."

"Have you really come here to discuss books and politics?"

With a surrendering smile, Ki said, "I'd like to know if you have any idea why three men who work for Miss Starbuck, the witness in your case, would have been murdered."

"Murder?" Her face settled from one of apparent surprise to one of knowing cynicism. "Of course . . . I'm sorry to hear that. It's as plain as day, though. Miss Starbuck is the only person who could get me acquitted. It sounds like Vargas has plans for her."

"What kind of plans?"

She seemed unsure, perhaps evasive, but the threat of her remark loomed large. She warned Ki to be very careful, night and day, but was unable to be specific. Consistently her refrain was about the power and ruthlessness of the Vargas family throughout recent history; how committed to ruining each other she, herself, and Wilfredo were. When Ki asked her to give examples, to verify suspicions about the Vargases that were held by many, she reiterated the story of how her father first had lost his land and then lost his life. Emmet Sykes had no enemies—except Vargas—and Leslie saw the timing of her father's murder as further proof of Vargas' absolute disregard for public opinion and the law. Although Ki, too, suspected Vargas of being capable of such arrogant outlawry, he contested, pointing out that Vargas's claim was so thoroughly substantiated as to be authentic beyond question. To Leslie, that was merely another example of Vargas's far-reaching power to get things done, his way. She had no doubt that his claim to her father's land and the land of many others was a fraud of unprecedented proportions.

She grew excited as she spoke, and her anger seemed to leap like tongues of fire from the windows of her eyes. She raced through her words, as if running out of time. Although never rising from the bed where she sat, her movements were expansive, filling the cell, especially her strong hands. Her short-trimmed fingernails and sun-tinted skin indicated an active woman, unafraid of work. In a gesture that brought her eyes rolling toward the ceiling, her arms circled upward. As her long lace sleeves fell back in mid-stretch Ki spied a curious gray blotch on her left wrist, then locked his eyes on hers again, before she noticed them wandering.

The accusations she made about the Vargas family were bewildering. As further evidence of the power Vargas wielded, she suggested that his corrupting influence infested even the nation's capital. In broad terms and with a steadily rising voice, she asserted that Vargas even helped instigate the Desert Land Act, passed by Congress in '77, as part of a two-pronged plot to usurp vast tracts of land west of the 100th meridian. By that law, any settler could buy a minimum of 640 acres if he would irrigate within three years. He was obliged to make a down payment of twenty-five cents per acre and, upon complying with the irrigation requirement, could buy the claim for a dollar more per acre.

"So here's Vargas with plenty of money to spare," she cried with growing agitation, speaking faster and more loudly with every word. "He claims five, six, ten square miles at a time, pays his two bits, spills a cup of water on it, and claims it's irrigated! The brilliance of the bloody thing is, the law doesn't specify any limit. No maximum! Of all the folks who come out this way, who can afford to irrigate anything at all, never mind pay for a minimum of six hundred and forty acres? It's only people like Vargas. It's criminal! The whole thing is even more despicable because huge amounts of the money Vargas put up for this came from corrupt foreign investors and industrialists!" With an emphatic finger thrust into her opposite palm she said, "After spending over a year in Europe looking into it, I know this for fact. I've met people and seen things that would make Vargas cower. He's a usurper of the lowest kind, and I can prove it."

Her words struck Ki like thunder. This Desert Land Act was not the everyday ring of rustlers or road agents. It represented a cabal that was far more evil and insidious, if only for seeming so innocent, so legal, having the approval of Congress and the cooperation of wealthy land barons. Ki knew that the average settler wouldn't pay for land that could be had free through the Homestead and Timber Culture acts. He had heard of ranchers exploiting the laws by paying the small down payment, grazing their stock for a few years, then vanishing without buying a square foot. After all, they could sell the beefers for a tenfold profit. Other cattlemen and speculators were laying claims, then selling or renting parcels they didn't own to gullible

24

grangers. But Vargas had gone even beyond the most extravagant sham anyone had tried yet, and he was winning. If the land fraud Miss Sykes accused him of proved true as well, the greed of such a man—such a dynasty—as Vargas was unfathomable.

Miss Sykes's year in Europe had commenced almost immediately after returning from the English boarding school her father had struggled to afford. No sooner had she come home—it was early summer just over eighteen months ago—than her father was taken from the earth forever. Convinced it was murder and that Vargas was behind it, she returned to Europe. Nearly her entire stay was spent plumbing the chaotic records in the ministries and government houses of Spain, from Madrid to Seville to Málaga and back, investigating Vargas's land claim. She now professed to have sure proof of its fraudulence, and was, therefore, more of a threat to the entire Vargas empire than merely the killer of Antonio Vargas. Before she said it herself, Ki realized that was the reason she was so disinclined to flee or bargain for her freedom. Jail was the safest place she could be.

Ki was fairly stunned and impressed. If this woman could be called calculating, it was a compliment. Her sense of justice and righteousness may have demanded an eye for an eye, but she was the one wronged—cheated, in fact, of seven thousand acres, a source of livelihood, income, and pride, and robbed of the only family she had in the world. The last living heir of her line, she had nothing to inherit.

"If Marx says anything in that book that makes good sense to me," Leslie continued, "it's the inevitability of conflict, especially where money is concerned, and why people who are in a fix, as I am, must hasten events to make things come their way.

"I don't know exactly why those men were murdered," she said, "but I'm fairly certain it was not a random act. You tell your friend Jessica Starbuck to be very careful."

Ki nodded solemnly to his feet. He started to thank her for what she had plenty enough to give—time—

25

when rising with him, she placed a warm hand upon his.

"I hope you'll be most careful, as well, Ki." Her hazel-eyed gaze was steady. Ki memorized every curve to her plush pink lips and small nose. Her hair had the luster of polished mahogany in the lamplight, and when she smiled, the thin ribbon of white teeth between her lips seemed to make the entire image shine. She moved closer until Ki felt the soft pressure of her full, round breasts against his forearm.

"As I said before, Ki, I am not a dreamer, I'm a doer. But I do have dreams. I hope you'll return safely and come see me again, perhaps soon."

Ki's heart fluttered to hear exactly the words he hadn't dared to hope for. He was never the type to miss such an opportunity. Taking her hand in his, he told her his return was assured, even if it meant seeing her behind bars. She laughed with brilliant eyes.

"The worst part is having to ask General Barefeet to close the curtain when I need privacy. Do you think he'll get suspicious if I ask him while you're visiting?"

"No," Ki replied, "but jealous for sure."

"Until you come for real, you'll come in my dreams."

The double meaning of her words wasn't lost on him.

Before Ki finished recounting his meeting with Leslie Sykes, Jessie sliced the air with her hand and announced, "We're leaving. That's it." She paced the room while figuring what needed to be done in order to leave Sarah promptly and return to the Circle Star. She instructed Ki to settle their debt with Widow Pritchard, but he tried to discourage her from her decision. If Leslie's warnings were substantial, Ki realized that Jessie would be endangered regardless of where she went. But Jessie would not be deterred. With the added protection of a couple of trusted guns she was confident that the Circle Star was the strongest place to take a stand. Swinging her saddlebag out from under the bed, she began packing. They would be ready to leave at first light. She thanked Ki for his suggestions, for looking at things from every direction and balancing her decisions. But this time something inside her said, *Go*.

Outwardly, their decision to put Sarah behind them showed nothing obvious. No announcement, no last-minute purchases, no hurrying up stairs or down alleys. But there were some folks then in Sarah whose keen observation of the Lone Star duo took notice of the inward momentum of their decision—certain folks, like the swarthy man who had sat near Jessie at Boney's and who watched attentively the reenactment she and Barefoot performed behind the hotel, knew the workings of minds like hers, knew the torment she was undoubtedly experiencing. And so they knew her plans.

★

Chapter 3

The whore knocked softly, as if she were wearing gloves. Any place else it would be viewed as a courtesy to the guests in adjacent rooms, it being well after midnight. But here, at the Longhorn Inn, such courtesies didn't apply. It was a flea-infested hovel with eighteen dingy, worn-out rooms barely large enough to swing a cat and probably with a whore in every one. Her knocking was answered by a man's voice so crackling it sounded like he couldn't clear the phlegm.

"Door's open."

A sickening yellow lamp light suffused the drab hallway, so when the door creaked open, the whore was but a silhouette seen from inside the unlit room. A narrow shard of light broke across the bed where one hairy forearm lay atop the bedspread. Between thick fingers was a crooked roll of tobacco, smoldering. The hand rose and vanished in the dark. A point of orange light flared in the darkness, then dimmed.

"You gonna stand there?" said the congested voice amid a swirl of smoke in the ray of light. The woman entered. She stood awhile until her eyes adjusted to the dark, then began to undress.

"It's two dollars minimum," she said, "five dollars all night. We can discuss the rest. What'll it be?" She heard the rush of an exhale.

"There's a half eagle by the basin. What's your name?"

"Crystal."

"I mean your real name, fer crissakes." When no answer came, he grumbled, "I don't get screwed except I know who's screwin' me; so if your name's more important than the gold, you can get out and screw yourself."

Quickly she answered, "Sherry—Sherry Vincent."

"God bless you, Sherry" was the man's reply.

He doused his fag when she stood naked at the foot of the bed. She was no beauty, but all right, he figured. Small, with a barrel torso and short brown hair framing a round face and a recessive jaw. The type to have more than one chin before she was thirty. She was wide in the hips and small in the tits, *Made to screw, not nurse,* he thought. Her eyes were set too close together. The narrow triangle of pubic hair looked thin and uninteresting. Her top-heavy thighs tapered rapidly to small knees and feet that were better off kept in the air.

She noticed something moving beneath the bed sheet. He was stroking himself. "Got any liquor?" asked the whore.

She heard the clink of glass and the splash of liquid, then the man's voice. "Here y'go."

As she came along the bedside he was disappointed that her ass was so flat and droopy, but he'd make do. She took the glass and sipped, trying to make out his face. All she could see was bristlelike hair at the top of his head, like some Indians she'd seen. He was sitting against the wall, head leaned back. She slipped one arm under the blanket. "Here, let me do that for you."

The man let out a long grunt and placed his glass on the bedside table. He sunk down further on the

29

strap-sprung bed, and his hips began to rock as the whore's tentative touch became firmer, more confident. His breathing deepened as she began stroking him in earnest, and she moaned with pretended sweetness between sips of whiskey. Releasing her grip momentarily, she slid her warm palm heavily down the length of his erection to his balls and gently grabbed them, moving them upward. The man's iron fist clamped tightly around her wrist.

"No," he insisted. "Never grab my balls."

He placed her hand back upon his penis, and she resumed stroking it slowly, squeezing it tightly at its base and stretching the skin on the upstroke. Placing her drink down, she lifted away the blanket and held the engorged shaft straight up. Nasty groans bubbled out of the man's chest as she bent his cock down toward his legs, then held its tip in her palm and rubbed it with a circular twist.

Picking up her drink again, she knocked it back, swallowing it in two loud gulps. She put the glass down and turned more fully toward the subject at hand. Her free hand stroked his rock-hard stomach, rippled like a washboard. His pecks were round and equally solid, and she flicked his small nipples to his increased delight. Squeezing downward his thick, swollen thing until her hand was in his pubic hair, she dropped her open mouth upon the sleek, curved muscle, closed her wet lips firmly around it, and thrust herself upon it until he was buried deep in her hungry throat. She commenced lifting and dropping her head madly, shaking her head side to side as her drool began to flow down to her firmly gripped fist.

His hands began to rove across her thighs until he felt the warmth of her pubis. Instinctively she widened her legs. Withdrawing his hand, he placed several knobby fingers into his mouth, slavering them generously, and forced his way between her labia, driving carelessly inside her. The woman flinched slightly but didn't miss a stroke. His fingers were gnarled branches, thick with calloused knots, with bark for

30

skin and tipped with broken, jagged nails. He jabbed again, eliciting a pained groan from her.

"Easy, that hurts," she said, then resumed bobbing her head upon him.

Kicking the covers from his legs, he guided her to straddle him. She crouched on the balls of her feet and guided his impatient rod in as she lowered herself. With both hands grasping her ass, he helped lift her upon strong, lean arms. He thrust his hips up to meet her, and their flesh was soon slapping loudly in time to the bedspring creaks. He stared intently at his rigid shaft penetrating deep into her pelvis, and they bucked until her knees became weak and she grew heavy in his arms. Whimpering gasps that could have been either pain or pleasure escaped from her thin lips, and her eyes were tightly shut.

Soon she could rise no more. Resting on her knees, she rocked, then angled her hips forward and back, bending his stiff shaft in a way that made the gruff man groan. Without withdrawing, he rolled over and flipped her on her back and started in ramming her. She opened her eyes.

Shock and dread bordering on panic filled her soul at the sight of his head in the midnight dark. Indistinct though it was, she could discern how the bristles at the top of his skull ended in a line curving from front to back high over his left ear. The entire side of his head was bare and shiny like wax, with the wormy texture and pale hue of scar tissue, wrinkled in some places and thicker in others. Distraught with fear, she shut her eyes again and considered trying to escape, but she hesitated and was soon convinced that this bizarre-looking man was no threat, that this was just another bizarre night's work.

Sitting back, he hooked his arms behind her knees and lifted them, spreading her wide. Up on his hands and toes, he thrust into her repeatedly, drawing her back into the moment. Involuntarily, she gasped, "Yes . . . yes!" His breath came more quickly; his pounding became more insistent. She reached down to their union and wrapped her fingers round his shaft, tightening them around it like a noose of pleasure, milking his cock for everything it was worth until, with an explosive bellow, he jetted copiously inside her, burying himself to the balls until every last jot was injected and every convulsion ceased.

He leaned back to catch his breath, not yet withdrawing. He cursed as if in disbelief. Wiped his forehead and lips. Finally rising, he doused his face with icy water from the washbasin, then returned. After a very few minutes he turned the whore onto her side. To her amazement he was erect again, and lifting her leg, he said, "Yeah, I'm ready for more. Let's go." He guided himself into her drenched pussy from behind and as he picked up the pace said, "You're gonna work for that gold, Sherry. Lord knows, you're gonna earn it."

It was still pitch-black outside when the sleeping whore was stirred by motion in the room. In dim lamplight the stranger with the hideously scarred head was dressing at the foot of the bed. Three times he had had his way with her, each time more prolonged, more perverse. His body was wiry and fit as a panther, but plug-ugly from the neck up. Primitive tattoos blackened his arms and shoulder. He pulled a pair of formal black slacks over his muscular thighs and noticed she was awake.

"You ain't from 'round here," he said. His gravelly throat apparently never cleared.

"You ain't neither," the whore yawned.

"I kin tell from the way you talk," he said. "You from back east, ain't ya? Where from?"

"Wilmin'ton," she muttered. "Nawth Ca'lina."

"What you doin' here, messin' with dudes like me?"

She snuggled into a more comfortable position. "It's a livin'."

The stranger snorted and buttoned his neat black shirt. Shiny black shoes and stockings to match. It gave her a creepy feeling.

"You some kinda unnertaker or sumpin?"

He snickered while tying his shoes. "Y'might say that . . . Where's your man? What's he do?" he asked.

The whore unconsciously touched her small gold wedding band. She felt exposed by the stranger's observation.

"Back east, in Wilmin'ton," she said meekly. "He's a law officer."

"Ha!" the stranger cackled. He faced the mirror and attached a collar. When he turned around, he presented himself with a big smile, wearing a priest's collar and a crucifix for the stunned woman to see. He raised his palms, then quickly threw on a long black coat. He gathered up a small satchel and headed for the door, where he paused. Waving his hand in the sign of the cross, he said, "Your husband must be one godawful asshole, but I'd be obliged to have communion with you again someday soon. *Adios.*"

Outside, a bitter wind went through his thin pants like they were gauze. He could barely see the street in front of him, it was so dark. He headed toward Broward's, the only pub in town that always kept a lamp burning. Rounding the corner of the building, he was startled by a hand against his shoulder. Reflexively, his iron grip seized the wrist and threw the stalker against the building, but before the scar-headed priest could do anything, there was a large fluted knife at his throat, held by the swarthy man who had been keeping his eyes on Jessie these past two days.

"Buenas noches, Señor Swann," said the knifeman. "I theenk I find you here, and *seguro,* I am right."

"Rojas! What the hell you doin', you dumb tur—"

The knife edge pressed deeper. Swann felt a trickle of warm blood turning cold as it dripped down his Adam's apple.

"Qué señor?"

Swann bit his lip and said, "You just scared the shit outta me, is all. I didn't know it was you." Rojas lowered his blade and stared directly into the eyes of the taller man. Swann wiped his throat and looked at the red smear on his fingers. "What the hell you want?"

33

"We must talk. Where you like?"

Swann cursed, then tipped his head. "Broward's."

It was warm inside and dusty as a grain silo. The bare dirt floor was covered by several inches of sawdust that piled against the furniture like small drifts of snow. The Mexican pointed to a table farthest from the only three drunks still awake. He slapped ten cents on the bar, saying, "*Amigo! Dos cervezas, por favor,*" and joined Swann. Rojas wore a faint, taunting smile that made his high cheekbones shine.

"I know you are coming back someday, but no so soon. No standing on your feet. *Muerte* maybe, not alive."

Unable to look Rojas dead-on, Swann nervously said, "Look, I planned to come back and settle things all along. I swear. I'm here, ain't I? You don't understand—"

"No," Rojas interrupted, "*you* don' understand." He crossed himself. "*Senor* Antonio—God rest his soul—he trust you. He help you. *Y tu?* You fly away like little bird. You no give him what you owe. *No pesos, no vacas—nada!*"

"I'm here!" Swann insisted. "I came back to settle things, to make things right."

"*Bueno! Bueno!*" Rojas said with open arms that nearly knocked the beer glasses from the approaching barkeep's hands. The torpid old man, as fat and bald as a shaved hog, had no reaction. He merely set them down and shuffled through the sawdust back to the card game, where one of the players was fast asleep.

"So," continued Rojas, eyeing Swann's collar, "you *padre* now? *Ave Maria!*"

Pulling on the front of his shirt, Swann drawled, "Naw, these are just something I picked up in Las Cruces."

"Ah, *si,* and you pick up nothing more? No gold cup? No jewel cross?" He leaned across the table. "I know you very well, *senor*. The *padre* that wore thees shirt, he no need shirts no more. But you need to pay money that you owe. Where are the gold cup and jewel cross?"

"Lay off, Rojas. That was weeks ago. Money don't last forever."

"Nor will you, *senor*, believe me." Rojas lifted his beer and guzzled down several mouthfuls at once. White foam clung to his black mustache as the glass hit the table.

"*Senor* Swann," Rojas said, "Don Antonio would haff kill you if he was alive, God rest his soul. But—Don Wilfredo, he want this money you owe very bad, and he give you the chance to get it."

"But that's exactly why I came back, don't you see? I was gonna—"

"*Merde!*" Rojas spat back. "You come back because you *loco in cabeza*. When Comanche scalp you, you lose some brain, too. You too much *estupido*."

"Go to hell, Rojas."

"No, you go to hell! You the one who will die if you not do as Don Wilfredo say, and I will haff honor to cut your worthless throat."

In the tense silence the two men sat back on their bare wood benches. Rojas took another long draft of beer. For someone of his small stature he had more brass than the navy and was as quick as a rattler. Even C. J. Swann, who would just as soon disembowel someone as shake his hand, knew better than to tangle with him. Besides, as much as he'd like to off the little Mexican prick, it was a sure thing that Vargas would just send someone else after him, and with greater vengeance. There weren't any options.

"What does he want me to do?" Swann asked.

"For thees," Rojas said, "you will need help—one, maybe two men. Someone must disappear for a while, but *mira . . .*" He raised one finger. "*Es mucho importante*: she must no be killed. Don Wilfredo does no want this woman to be harm. Only that she disappear a little while. If something go wrong"—the emphatic pause and pointed finger made Swann hold his breath—"it will be you life. *Comprende?*"

Swann lifted his glass for the first time and emptied it all at once. He ran his sleeve across his stubbly face

35

and burped, nodding his head in affirmation.

"Yeah. I git it. You tell Vargas don't worry. What do I get in return?"

"*Ay coño, hombre, qué estupido!*" Rojas sang out with a grimace. "Your *life* you get!"

Outside, nearly half an hour later, the sky was brightening. Sparrows were beginning to twitter. Swann raised the collar on his coat, and Rojas chuckled.

"Ees good to cover your collar, *padre*. Someone recognize you, they no believe in God no more."

As Rojas swaggered away, Swann took a deep breath and cursed his luck. He had barely paid attention to Rojas' instructions, he was so nervous; but he understood that Rojas would pay two hundred dollars in gold to each man Swann hired on. All Swann would get was what he had already, his life, and that angered the scar-headed reverend. *That'll have to change*, he swore to himself. *I ain't workin' for nothin' while somebody else is gettin' paid in gold.* He was glad Rojas didn't attempt to cut him. It would have been bad ugly. Like two vicious polecats fighting it out in a cage. He organized his thoughts and figured what he had to do, whom he had to see. He'd have to move fast.

Tatum lived in a ramshackle cabin on the outskirts of town. It was surrounded by the sorriest-looking hog pens in Texas, unkempt shit holes that smelled so bad they'd make vomit seem edible. Swann tried not to gag as he stepped up to the rickety door and tried the latch. It was unlocked. He stepped in quietly.

Inside, the messy two-room place didn't smell much better than outside. What little furniture Tatum had was salvaged and pieced together with wire, rope, and nails. Limp brown cloth covered the windows, and it was hellishly cold. Heading for the back room, Swann sent an empty whiskey bottle rattling away in circles with his foot.

"Tatum?" he said.

He stepped forward and pushed the half-open bedroom door wide.

"Tatum?"

Glass shattered against the door near his hand, peppering his face with needle-sharp fragments. Someone cursed, shadows moved, a chunk of firewood came flying and deflected off the doorpost.

"Who are ya'?" Tatum yelled from his bed. "Who's there, goddamn it?"

Swann yelled back, "You dumb shit, it's me!" and cautiously poked his head in the door. A silver glint flashed before his eyes. He flinched, but felt a cold stripe of blood stretch across his cheek. "Shit!" he yelled, and before he could look back, Tatum crashed into him, bowling him down backward on the littered floor, trying to bury a blade in Swann's chest, when suddenly Tatum recognized the scarred head. His eyes widened in terror. He cursed and leaped to his feet and bolted for the front door.

Swann reached for his ankles. "C'mere, you idjit!" he grunted. He caught a pant leg and held fast with two fingers. Tatum hit the floor chin first, rolled over, and began kicking like a child at Swann, who scrambled up his leg for a better hold.

Like a scrawny yelping dog, Tatum cried, "Git off me! Git off me!" and swiped his knife blade back and forth before Swann's face, never daring to get close enough to slice him a second time.

"Goddamn it, Tatum, shut up! I ain't gonna kill ya, I swear! I got a goddamn job fer ya!"

The kicking and swinging slowly ceased. Tatum propped himself on his knobby elbows, with one foot poised to strike.

"A job?" he gasped, with chest heaving.

On his knees, Swann mumbled in his phlegmy voice, "That's what I said. One hundred bucks in gold, you shit, and it ain't like you deserve it, neither."

"Y'ain't gonna kill me?"

Swann slapped Tatum's thigh and dragged himself to his feet.

"Not right now, you horse's ass! If I was fixin' to kill ya, I'd be eatin' yer liver fer breakfast right now. Git up! We got some figgerin' to do."

★

Chapter 4

Widow Pritchard's sourdough bread went down well with her freshchurned butter and coffee, even if Jessie had to brew it herself so early in the morning. When she and Ki were done eating, the sun still wasn't high enough to be seen over nearby rooftops, glowing a grayish yellow through a thick cloud cover. Ki still had a bag to pack, so Jessie volunteered to fetch the horses from the livery. Afterward, she and Ki were expected to meet Brant Adams and Howie Judd, their armed escorts, in front of the marshal's office.

With her thick fleece collar turned up against her cheeks Jessie scurried across the rear courtyard. The sky looked miserable, but she knew it wasn't likely to get any worse. Had it been a few months earlier, she might have wondered whether such skies announced the coming of "El Niño," the weeks-long storm that drowns half the state every few years. Most times, skies like these were just threats.

The tall door to the stables wouldn't budge when Jessie pulled. She got a better grip and tried again, but it was locked from inside, and things sounded pretty quiet. No hammering or raking, no talking. Just the sound of hoofs on packed earth and an occasional snort.

Surprised that no stablemen were there yet, Jessie decided to head back to the hotel. The town was beginning to come alive, and Jessie saw a few people pass along the main street on foot or horseback. Halfway across the yard she changed course, deciding to walk down to meet Adams and Judd. She slipped down an alley beside Whittaker's. Emerging at the far end, she stopped short to avoid colliding with a tall man walking with his head down. He wore a wide-brimmed black hat that shielded his face from the wind. Between his lapels she saw his collar and crucifix.

"Pardon me, Reverend," she said.

He touched his brim, said, "Mornin'," and they both kept walking.

Far behind her two men staggered out of Broward's tavern. One of them stumbled into the street, trying to keep his feet as he crossed the frozen ruts. Seeing the reverend across the way, he chuckled and said, "Howdy, Reverend. Good mornin' to ya."

The stubbly face beneath the brim leered long enough for the drunk to observe the lack of hair over the left ear.

"Hey!" the drunk called out. "C.J.? That you?" His cackling laugh wouldn't have been enough to attract Jessie's attention from down the way, but when he said, "Now what in tarnation you all gussied up like that for, Ceej? Ha! You a preacherman now?" Jessie looked back. The minister waved the old drunk off and continued along his way, leaving the drunk to shake his head and laugh about the hallucination his lifetime of hard drinking had obviously created. The drunk tried to explain the sight to his partner, who wanted nothing to do with him either. Jessie walked on.

Adams and Judd were having a smoke beside their tethered horses when Jessie arrived. She explained

39

why she was on foot, and together they walked back up to Pritchard's hotel. Before passing Whittaker's, Jessie tried the front door of the livery again, only to find it still locked tight. She asked the men if they'd like to warm their bones with a pot of hot java and some of Widow Pritchard's sourdough, and Adams rubbed his empty stomach in response.

The black-clad "reverend" had caught enough sight of Jessie to make his loins ache with lust. The long coppery hair that flowed from beneath her brown Stetson was a splash of dazzle in an otherwise drab landscape. The sway of her wide hips and plush butt were neither hidden by her long coat nor missed by his leering over-the-shoulder glance. *What a prize,* he thought.

He turned into the double doorway of the seedy Longhorn Inn. On the second floor, at the head of the wide, creaky stairway, he rapped loudly on the first door he came to.

"Dupree!" His voice crackled like a wet-wood fire. "Dupree! It's me, C.J. Wake up!"

A groggy voice replied, and Swann could hear the bedsprings flex as Dupree roused himself. The latch was thrown, and Dupree, draped in a bed sheet, took a squinting, disbelieving look at Swann. He was a handsome young buck with a square jaw and deepset, principled eyes. Beneath the folds of the sheet his well-defined muscles rippled with every move. He was a full head shorter than Swann, and what looked like a day's growth of beard was actually several month's worth. His fingernails were dirty and broken.

He mumbled, "I ain't never touching another drop o' that tangle-foot agin," and pulling the bed sheet tighter, he shuffled back to bed. Plopping onto the lifeless mattress, he said, "Some dumb ass must be paying you in gold for you to wear that cross—and don't get too close! I don't wanna die when you get struck by lightning."

"I got a job for ya," Swann said. "But we gotta git movin' right now. It's a simple, easy deal—no fussin', no killin', no robbin'. Real easy."

"I knew you couldn't have been coming to see me on no social call, C.J. Every time I see your ugly face, it's trouble. Forget it. You'd be better off as a hallelujah shouter. Shut the door behind you."

Swann refused to leave without him, and things looked like a standoff until he pulled the covers off Dupree's naked body. Dupree cursed and covered himself again. He was just over twenty, but still a child. Swann said he understood why he wouldn't want to get tangled up with him after what happened last time. Dupree was a two-time loser with a soft shell. The second time he got dragged down, pistol-whipped, and locked away for robbery, it was with C. J. Swann, and the two of them were damn lucky not to have ended like their other two partners, who were now fertilizing some pasture north of San Antonio. Swann even went so far as to admit being a little careless that time, not because of the way he planned things or the way he handled himself, but because he had hired those two greenhorns. Dupree sat up.

"Do I hear Charles Joseph Swann—the infamous "Caddo Jack" Swann—*apologizing* for messing up a bank job that nearly got me killed? I must be dreaming! Either that, or the squaw who scalped you took too much off the top."

Swann lurched forward and pinned Dupree down with a powerful single-handed choke hold.

"Shut up or I'll kill you here and now!" he hissed. After a moment he released his grip and threw Dupree's head to the pillow. He straightened his coat and paced the small room in tight circles. "Look. I've had two shit-ass sidewinders put knives to my face and one future dead man say what you just said to me already this mornin'. I don't cotton to no wet-behind-the-ears jackleg granger like you smart-mouthin' C. J. Swann like that. Y'hear?"

Coughing until his head turned purple, Dupree tried to keep his eyes on the unpredictable goat. He was determined to fight him if he had to, knowing full well what the outcome would likely be.

41

"Now," Swann said more calmly, "I ain't gonna let you work me up into no lather. I just come here 'cause I got nobody else, or believe me, I wouldn't waste my time with you. But I got no time for palaverin'. This here's the deal."

He recounted all the details—what needed to be done and with whom. He outlined everything Rojas had told him earlier, conveniently leaving out the fact that his own life wasn't worth a cow chip if they messed up. He also didn't want the kid to turn tail before getting fully involved, so he conveniently raised Rojas' offer to three hundred in gold right on the spot, for the sake of bringing Dupree aboard.

"Look," Swann said huskily, "this here's good money. Easy money. It's Vargas, and you know he's good for it. You've worked for him before. It's not even like you'd be working for me."

Dupree sat up, putting his feet on the cold wood floor. Swann could see how desperate the kid was. His brain was squirming, imagining what he could do, how far he could run, with three hundred dollars.

Swann turned up his palms, looking more like a preacher than ever.

"You're a tad gun-shy, is all. That's natural. You'll get over it soon as you git in the saddle agin."

"I don't want to get into no saddle with you again," Dupree replied. "All that killing's only gonna get me killed one day."

Swann's eye brows rose. "But that's just it, kid! Ain't no killin' this time. None! All we do is keep the lady outta sight a while, then let her go wherever she's hankerin' to go, once it's all blown over and Vargas gives us the word. It's simple!" He got no reaction from the kid, so he stood back and continued with another approach.

"Look at yourself, kid. You're broke. You done been dirt-poor broke all your life, and you're sick of it. Am I right? 'Cause if you ain't, you're just plain sick. How long you gonna punch them dogs for them few bits a day, bustin' your back for them ranchers that don't give a piss about you? How much o' that odd-job shit can you do for the scraps them landowners throw you before you git so damn riled you just wanna blow their goddamn empty heads right off their shoulders, huh? This is easy money, kid! The easiest you're likely to find. But I gotta know *now*."

Dupree stared at him, obviously wanting to agree but scared.

"I ain't gonna kill no one, C.J."

"You don't got to."

"I don't even want to carry a gun."

Swann shrugged. "You don't got to."

The kid shook his head, disappointed with himself. He stood and pulled on his leather-patched woolens in silence.

"I oughta be hog-tied for getting mixed up with the likes of you," he mumbled.

The pot of coffee was nearly empty when Jessie walked up to her room to carry down her saddlebags. It had been more than an hour since she last tried the door at the livery stable without luck. Somebody must have been sick or sleeping in, she figured. Hoisting the leather across her shoulder, she peered out the window into the courtyard below one last time. Across the yard a man approached the rear door to the stable, pulled the handle, and it opened. *It's about time,* she thought.

While Adams and Judd waited in the warm sitting room at Pritchard's, Jessie and Ki walked to the stable, irritated by their late start. When they tried the door, again it was locked.

"Hello!" Jessie called, banging the heavy door with her open hand. "Anybody in there? Open up already. It's late!" She threw Ki an exasperated glance. He walked up the alley to try the front door. She heard him slam the wood with his powerful hand and call, then he was at the corner of the building, beckoning her to come up front.

A scrawny, scruffy hostler took his sweet time opening the wide stable door and unlocking another. He didn't look all too bright, and he halfheartedly excused

43

himself by claiming not to be an early riser.

"Where's Mister Stewart?" Jessie asked. The skinny man looked surprised. "John Stewart?" she repeated. "The owner?"

"Oh! Stewart!" the hostler cried out. "I thought you said 'Calvert.' These ears ain't what they used to be neither, not since I took a howitzer blast right close to my head onc't. Injun attack, you know. Terrible fierce, and besides, there ain't no Calvert, so far as I know, in these here parts, no, ma'am."

"Who are you?" Ki asked. "I don't think I've ever seen you around."

The man's eyebrows seemed pinned high to his forehead. "Tatum. Just ol' Tatum. That's what folks call me."

A pregnant silence followed, which Tatum didn't seem inclined to disturb, so Jessie said, "We're here to collect our rigging and our horses. The name's Starbuck. Would you kindly fetch them, please?"

" 'Course, ma'am." But the smiling fool remained where he stood.

Ki stepped very close to the man. Tatum's nose practically touched his chin. His words came one at a time.

"Tatum. Go. Get. Our. Horses. Now." When Tatum still didn't budge, Ki added, "Or I. Will pull. Your heart. Out. Through. Your mouth. Okay?"

Nodding fast and twitching like an insect, Tatum stammered, " 'Course! And what was your names agin?"

Jessie and Ki exchanged amazed glances.

She said, "Are we still in bed dreaming this?"

Ki stood close to him again, saying, "Starbuck. Jessica Starbuck. Hers is the steeldust gelding. Mine is the grulla mare. Now move!"

He turned the dolt by his shoulders and shoved him forward. All Tatum could do was wander aimlessly among the stalls, repeating the name "Starbuck," and poking his nose at the horses to see what he could see. Walking back from the rear of the building, he paused halfway along and shouted, "Say, just what is a

44

steeldust anyhow?" at which point Ki strutted toward him in exasperation. Ki's demeanor was threatening enough to cause Tatum to back away, and his rambling excuses were barely comprehensible.

"That one . . ." Ki said, pointing into one stall, "and that one," pointing into another. "Get 'em out and get 'em saddled, or get yourself a new job after I have a word with Stewart."

Tatum yessed him abundantly as he opened the stalls and led the animals to Ki, then scampered off to look for their rigging. He rummaged around the building for so long that Jessie was beside herself. She yelled out the fool's name and went to him when he answered.

"Just what in heaven's name are you doing here? Where is Mr. Stewart?"

"Oh, well, Stewart couldn't git here today, ma'am. Feeling under the weather, he was. The rheumatiz, I hear, terrible bad. I'm just helping out fer the day or so."

"Do know what a saddle looks like?"

"Oh, sure, sure," he laughed. "Use 'em all the time, sure."

"Mine is a rimfire with strings and conchas. Okay? Some embossing on the fenders and behind the cantle. I'd appreciate it if you look real hard and real fast."

Tatum raised his hand and assured her he knew just the one she described and flew off behind a partition wall. When he came back, he carried a three-quarter kidney pad befitting a know-nothing pilgrim on a wind-broke, pus-gutted goat. Jessie lost it.

"Imbecile! Do you see any embossing or any conchas on that piece of hide? What's wrong with you? Ki!"

The black-haired warrior lurched forward and grabbed Tatum by the nape of the neck. Insisting they go take a look together, he drove the no-account polecat toward the tack again, forcing him to stumble over the saddle he let fall. Suddenly Tatum resisted and tried to throw Ki's hand off, but Ki's grip became

45

viselike, and with his other hand he touched a little-known pressure point that sent a warm shock through Tatum's body, enough to make him not dare another escape. Directly ahead of them sat Jessie's saddle and next to it, Ki's. The steel-fisted warrior shoved Tatum at one of them and ordered, "Carry that one out. I'll take the other." Before Tatum lifted the saddle from its rail, a door to the loft swung open.

"Can I help you?"

It was Dupree, and when he turned his sparkling eyes and sculpted features toward Jessie, they both took second glances. Dupree's breathing was heavy after descending only a flight of stairs, and his face was a little too flushed. He thought fast on his feet and sized up the situation quickly. He had an innocent face that made lying easy.

"Is there a problem, sir? Ma'am?" he asked.

When the explanation came, Dupree scolded Tatum, who was much older than he. Dupree hefted Ki's saddle and dressed the grulla with apologies, doing a good, fast job of it. When he was done, Jessie asked what she owed him, but he declined payment on account of the poor service.

Folding his hands together in front of him like a well-trained schoolboy, Dupree gushed, "I'm real sorry my cousin done caused you so much trouble. He hasn't been the same since"—he leaned a little closer and whispered—"since the fever took him after that fall he took from some ornery old bronc. He's a little . . . you know . . ." He twirled a finger near his temple. "But, like he said, Mr. Stewart's a tad under the weather, and since we've been staying at his house an all—I'm his nephew, y'see—I was obliged to see to his affairs. He's a right generous man, my uncle. Why, he protested till he was red in the face, but I just wouldn't hear it. No, ma'am. So he's just restin' up some. I'm sure he'll be up an' around in a day or two. I'll be sure to tell him you came by and was asking for him. He'll be a might sunnier hearin' that, I'm sure. I 'ppreciate y'all comin' by. Y'all travel safe now. Bye-bye."

Leading the animals by the reins to the hotel, Ki glanced over his shoulder cautiously. He suggested they quit the town as fast as possible; too many things weren't right in Sarah. Rejoining Adams and Judd, they mounted with weapons loaded. Bidding Widow Pritchard farewell, they headed for the road that would take them home.

As soon as Dupree had closed the stable door, Tatum rushed up behind him and shoved him hard into the wood.

"What in tarnation you think you doin', treatin' me like some little grubeater and making out like I'm loco?" He pushed him again, but Dupree easily fended him off. "What was all that? I was doin' just fine."

Locking a powerful hand on Tatum's twig of a wrist, Dupree said, "Stifle it. There's no time for your mule-headed nonsense. Saddle up."

It wasn't long before they were ready to ride. As soon as Dupree saw Jessie and her companions heading out of town, he hurried to the loft upstairs. In the hay close by a wall lay a white-haired man, gagged and tied at the wrists and ankles. A rivulet of blood trickled from his scalp. Dupree looked around and lifted his war bag from near the top of the stairs. From it he removed a large knife. The man's eyes grew wild with fear as its nicked edge hovered menacingly above him. Dupree knelt beside him, raised the blade above his shoulder, and thrust it down into the floorboard flush against the wall, its jagged edge standing exposed. With a leather thong he lashed the handle securely to an iron spike jutting from the wall stud and knotted it tightly.

Turning intently to the terrified man, he said, "I apologize for that knot on your head, Mr. Stewart, but I want you to know it was an accident. I ain't gonna hurt you, like I promised. Now this here knife, all you gotta do is shimmy yourself around and rub against it to cut the ropes. We just need some time before you go fetchin' folks after us. I sure hope you understand: I ain't no killer, and I don't wish you no harm."

47

He took his bag and started down the steps, pausing to give Stewart a last look and a nod of assurance. The old farrier closed his eyes and thanked his stars, feeling sorry for this kid who, he was sure, would come to no good.

★
Chapter 5

Not far out of Sarah the gravelly road that would bring Jessie and Ki home to the Circle Star Ranch left behind the level plain, with its groves of trees and meandering creeks, and climbed gentle slopes that formed the foothills of the mountains to the west. On a clear day Jessie could see the slumbering blue-gray giants on the horizon stretching north and south in a majestic, if broken, chain. But today, thick, ominous clouds hovered low to the ground, billowing angrily as if prepared to belch their stormy innards upon the world below and prevent anything more than a few short miles away from being seen. She knew that the skies in these parts could look that way for weeks and nothing but cold ever come of it.

Adams and Judd paired off at the rear, keeping their eyes roving over the brown and golden terrain. In the distance they noticed the land became furrowed and more varied in color, dotted with the broken ledges and odd formations that were badlands. They talked quietly about mundane things—corral gates, barbed wire, and burns taken while branding beeves. They packed nearly matching rifle scabbards and, one man being right-handed and the other a lefty, had them strung across opposite skirts. Adams toted a twenty-year-old Henry "Yellow Boy" that looked like it was cast the day before. On its polished butt stock was a brass escutcheon bearing his initials. Judd, being an avid sport shooter, packed his pride and joy, a 34-inch, .44-100 Creedmoor, among Remington's finest. Adams didn't like the idea of using a breechloader as a defensive weapon, but Judd, with his cartridge belt fully stocked, was the fastest, most accurate marksman this side of the Pecos. He didn't even own a pistol; this time he also carried a borrowed Remington No. 3, chambered for .44-40 Winchester. He wore it under his coat, slung on a lanyard from a swivel, feeling certain he wouldn't need it.

A few miles out, the road narrowed and dipped down beside an arroyo lined with dagger-sharp lechugilla and thick with creosote bushes. As the road curved around the bottom of the rocky slope Jessie and Ki moved out of Adams' and Judd's sight. It unsettled Adams, the older of the two, and he told his partner so. Judd was silent, but watchful.

"Better check," Judd said, and nudged his mount into a quicker pace. As he came around the curve to where a high wall of crumbling rock faced him there was no sign of Jessie or Ki.

"Brant!" he called, and jabbed his spurs into the broomtail's flank, drawing his Creedmoor as he fell into the animal's rhythm. The road appeared to veer off toward the arroyo, and as Judd cleared the embankment, with Adams coming up fast, he saw Jessie and Ki moving on peacefully where the road swung back the opposite way, behind the rock wall. Startled by the hoofbeats and by Judd's drawn rifle, Jessie drew her double-action Colt.

"Howie? What's wrong?" she asked excitedly.

Judd wasn't the type to be embarrassed by his own diligence, even when mistaken. His explanation won Jessie's thanks.

She replaced her weapon in its hogleg, not the most comfortable rig when riding, but trusted and well used. The Colt was a fine piece, a gift from her father years before. She carried it proudly—and it served her well more often than she cared to think. Alex Starbuck had taken great pains to ensure that his daughter could fend for herself, the result being a woman who could handle a smoke pole as well as most any man. Hers was a .38 caliber slate gray beauty, the color of that day's Texas sky. The polished peachwood grips and .44 frame were her father's choice, wise ones that reduced the pistol's recoil and allowed Jessie to outshoot her expert father in both speed and accuracy. A woman not to be trifled with.

"We'll water the horses at the spring up the road a piece," Jessie told everyone. "Just stay alert. The brush gets pretty thick; there's more places to hide."

Prickly pear crowded the well-worn trail that led to the watering hole. Further down, brittle sage gave way to creosote that grew to several feet high, studded here and there by the tall, barren flower stems of yucca and century plants swaying in the steady wind. Before descending, the four riders spread apart. Adams and Judd watched from the road above while Ki led the way down to the spring. The earth was coarse and crumbly. His horse faltered.

"Okay!" Ki called out. "Looks good."

Adams and Judd dismounted but stayed on the road. Ki stood vigilant as ever. Slipping off behind some bushes, Jessie removed her gun belt, dropped her drawers, and squatted to pee. Adams and Judd had the same need, and Judd went first, holding his loaded Creedmoor at his side the whole time. Just as his first yellow stream hit the dirt, something rustled through the creosotes behind the spring. Ki and Judd trained their eyes in that direction, but all was still. The stalk of a century plant several feet away swayed too much for it to have been the wind, and Ki drew his Peacemaker from the cross-draw holster on his hip. Judd calmly continued pissing, keeping one hand on his trousers, the other holding up the Creedmoor, eyes on the bushes. Adams stood by his mount several yards from Judd, with his back turned. His Yellow Boy remained in its rifle boot while he inspected the rigging on his mount, unaware anything was amiss. The only sounds for nearly a minute were the sadly moaning wind and rustle of the bushes. Ki could hear that Jessie had finished urinating.

A twig snapped near where she still crouched. The century plant shivered hard, and the dry grass crunched. Something moved. Jessie screamed as a dark bulk flew against her. Ki and Judd cocked and aimed their weapons simultaneously and waited for a target when suddenly from the underbrush burst four frightened javelinas, charging out of the arroyo and disappearing into the wilderness.

Their sighs of relief turned to laughter when Jessie stood amid the brush looking frightened and holding her open pants up to her hips, beneath her bunched-up overcoat. Breathlessly she cried, "The damn thing came right at me! Scared the daylights out of me!" The hammers on their guns clicked home softly.

Over the next few miles Ki had plenty of time to recount for Jessie Leslie Sykes's background and her theories regarding the murder of her father. Based on what she had heard about the Vargas family, Jessie had little doubt Miss Sykes was telling the truth. But murder is murder, no matter how you justify it.

"How soon after she returned from boarding school was her father killed?" Jessie asked.

Ki tried to get it straight in his own mind. "Vargas made his land claim about two years ago. So when Leslie returned home that May, she found her father already in deep trouble. Five or six weeks later he was dead and she was alone."

Left with nothing but her anger, Jessie thought.

Ki could read it in her face. He knew how intimately Jessie understood that feeling. Her eyes stared long into her past. In the silence between them the hoofbeat rhythm soon helped her melancholy pass and she came back to the present.

"I wonder what Wilfredo did with that gun he lifted from his father's body," she mused. "I'm certain Antonio fired that bullet in the tree."

Ki remembered something important.

"Leslie Sykes has a powder burn. I noticed it when I talked with her back there in the hoosegow."

Jessie perked up. "Where is it?"

"Left wrist."

Jessie slapped her thigh. "I knew it! Ki, I like the way that woman thinks." Ki seemed confused. "She thinks just like I do," she said proudly.

"Wagon up ahead!" Adams shouted.

A black spring buggy leaned over the road's edge, with one wheel low on the slope. A splayfooted paint stood across the narrow road tethered to a singletree that had seen better days. A man dressed entirely in black was trying to shake off the cold by stomping a cold-weather jig. When he saw the riders approaching, he flicked a butt of rolled tobacco into the brush and jammed his freezing hands into his coat pockets. From a good distance Jessie and Ki could see the white collar that marked him as a man of the cloth.

Adams and Judd kept their hands on their rifle butts despite the fact that this far out it was usually only missionaries or Circle Star ranch hands one would be likely to meet on this road. They slowed their pace as they neared the buggy.

"Trouble?" asked Ki.

In a choked voice that barely carried over the wind the reverend answered, "God bless y'all," and touched the wide brim of his hat. "I thought surely I'd be going to my reward tonight. Y'all are a welcome sight. Seems I got a mite close to the edge here, and—I guess I was startin' in to noddin'—and I reined the old nag in hard, but . . . she reared and acted up, tried to turn tail or something. Next thing I know, I hear this terrible sound, like wood cracking, and . . . well, here I am.

Lord be praised for you coming by. Hallelujah and amen!"

The hat pulled far down on the man's head was familiar to Jessie. *"Pardon me, Reverend"* . . . *"Now what in tarnation you all gussied up like that for, Ceej? You a preacherman now?"* She didn't know what to think of a minister out here by himself with this half-useless crowbait. Before she could ask anything, the gruff-voiced man beat her to it.

"If you know something about these things, I sure would be obliged. . . ."

Adams and Judd didn't want to appear threatening, but their hands were ready. With a confident nod toward Jessie, Ki moved to dismount.

The crack of a bullet. A puff of smoke from the preacher's coat. The head of Ki's horse jolted aside in a spray of blood. The animal toppled, pinning Ki under several hundred pounds of coyote feed. The two gun hawks went for their irons.

Jessie's mount reared. She kneed him into a tight reverse. Judd moved like lightning. Reining his mount into a quick sidestep, he brought the Creedmoor level, but Jessie's rearing mount blocked his shot. Adams' Henry repeater hadn't even cleared the scabbard before a shot rang out from behind, shattering his elbow within its sleeve. His weapon hit the ground. Jessie dug her spurs down hard to make a run for it but pulled back into a full stop upon seeing the black holes of Dupree's and Tatum's gun barrels staring at her like the eyes of death. Dupree spurred his sweating mount alongside her and snatched her Colt from its holster while Tatum held a trap-door Springfield carbine at her chest.

Judd was working the reins desperately when another shot from behind slammed into the receiver of his gun. The Creedmoor jumped from his hand. Instantly he reached for the Remington, forgetting he had closed a button on his coat. He yanked on the lanyard, but not fast enough.

"Don't touch it!" screamed Swann. He stood with his Russian cocked and aimed at Judd's head. The hired gun froze just as Swann caught sight of Ki pulling himself from under the twitching mare.

Swann spun and shot Ki square in the chest.

Jessie, Dupree, and Howie Judd simultaneously shouted in horror as the startled horses jumped. Judd pulled his coat open, the button popped and flew. He fumbled for the Remington. Swann, with jaw clenched, spun again and sent a chunk of hot lead burning straight through Judd's face.

"Goddamn son of a bitch!" Dupree yelled. "What in hell you doing?"

"Shut up! I'll kill you, too!" Swann bellowed. "They was drawin' on me, damn it. Tatum! You see that? Am I lyin'?" Tatum twitched his head for "no," and Swann said, "Now get them guns, and let's get a move on! *Now!*"

"Ki!" Jessie sobbed. "Oh, my God, Ki!" She started to dismount, but Swann leveled his gun at her.

"Stay in your saddle or die!"

Blood on the outside of Ki's coat seeped black in the mournful winter light. The whites of his eyes were slits beneath his parted eyelids, and one hand shook for moment, then stopped. "Ki!" Jessie screamed, and her body heaved with tearful sobs. She clamped her hands across her mouth, as if to prevent his courageous spirit from hearing her pitiful crying.

The brigands moved efficiently. Despite Dupree's worried complaining, Adams was pulled down from his mount and left to writhe in pain, certain to die, on the frozen ground. Swann ordered Dupree to unsaddle Judd's big-chested piebald while he produced a pack-saddle from inside the buggy. Tatum kept Jessie under the gun, his eyes bulging with eagerness. Swann and Dupree hefted several large sacks, hides, and bundles from the buggy and onto the racks, and after a lead rope was tied from the horn of Swann's saddle to the bridle of Jessie's broomtail, they were ready. Tatum's parting gesture was to bat Adams's horse and the bare-back paint on their buttocks with the stock of Adams' Yellow Boy, sending the animals wild-eyed into the cold. With a guttural yell from Swann they were on their way westward across trackless wilderness.

"You bastards!" Adams cried out after them, unable to lift himself from the stony ground. "By God, I swear I'll see you pay! I swear!"

His voice was soon lost in the shifting winds, though he yelled to exhaustion, watching helplessly as the riders receded into the limitless badlands ahead.

He broke down and cried. Cried hard enough to make up for the years he never allowed himself to cry. When he grew too weary to cry anymore, he looked around with a shiver that went to his very core. It would be dark soon and cold. He would probably die tonight. He cradled his shattered arm and lowered his head and prayed, asking for forgiveness, if not for help.

In the hour it took him to crawl behind the meager shelter of a large rock and two creosotes, he had worked up some body heat, but within minutes of sitting still, he was shivering uncontrollably. He tried to will the tremors to cease. For brief welcomed moments his muscles would relax, only to convulse again into rapid spasms. His helplessness offended him. Anger flooded his body and clouded his eyes. He cursed his killers and cursed his own wasted life.

"Goddamn!" he growled into the void. He looked skyward and yelled, "Why don't you hear me?"

A voice on the wind replied, "Oh, shit!"

"Wha'?" Adams cried. "Lord Awmighty, what was that? That you?"

"Oh, son of a bitch!"

He turned into the shifting wind with fearful surprise and saw Ki moving his arm, clutching his chest, trying to speak. Adams called out to him. Forgetting his own pain and cold, he scrambled around the fallen grulla, clutching his wounded arm to his body. He crouched beside Ki and shook him with his good hand.

"My chest," Ki groaned. "I'm shot."

Adams tore open Ki's coat and lifted his woolen shirt. A flattened piece of lead fell across the worn brown leather vest beneath. A halo of blood around the point of impact stained the clothing. Opening the vest, Adams found the inside to be lined with pockets. Each pocket was filled with several of the shiny metal throwing stars called *shuriken*, three of which, in the pocket behind the bullet holes through the outer clothing, were badly dented, and some of their razor-sharp points had lacerated Ki's breast.

"Why you dumb-luck son of a gun!" Adams cried. In his joy he grabbed a fistful of Ki's clothing, causing the wounded man to wince in pain. "Glory be, I ain't never seen nothing so—"

The realization that Ki's good fortune might not change anything cut Adams short. Ki was groggy from having slammed his head during his fall, and he'd have to be helped. Adams talked him along, lightly slapped his face, and shook him awake. Ki had trouble focusing his eyes and regaining his balance, but soon struggled to a sitting position. That's when he realized how cold he was.

"Brant," he sighed, "I thought I was a goner. That thing hit me like a falling building."

"Considerin' you bein' shot, and whackin' your noggin, and havin' a horse fall on top o' you, I'd say you're seeing things about right." Then Adams's face clouded over. His eyes wrinkled. "Howie—he weren't so lucky. They done shot him dead, Ki. Cold dead." Ki saw the soles of Judd's boots and his body lying in a heap. "Goddamn, Ki. How'm I gonna tell his brother?"

Ki shook his head. "Are they gone?" he asked.

Adams nodded. When he was about to tell Ki about the horses, he spotted his own, grazing a hundred yards beyond the buggy.

"Ki!" he prodded, trying to lift him to his feet, "Ki! You gotta get up. C'mon, hoss, I can't do this myself. We gotta catch that critter if we're gonna get back alive and find them drygulchin' bastards!"

Ki's knees were weak. It seemed to take forever to climb to his feet, and only a second to fall again. His dizziness made him little help. Fortunately, Adams's mount seemed content despite the cold and stood still long enough for Adams to finally take the reins. His pain was excruciating, but so was his fear of dying in the cold. The gun hawk looked worried.

"It's hours back to Sarah," he said to Ki. "We might freeze to death before we get back."

The ponytailed warrior wavered on his feet. "No. We'll stop and build a fire, rest up some. We'll get there, Brant. If I have to lasso the whole damn town from here and drag it to us, I swear we'll make it, on Jessie's life."

★
Chapter 6

"Gimme the Overholt."

Swann never looked at anyone he was addressing unless he had to, which confused Dupree and Tatum to no end. They looked at each other, wondering who the order was intended for. The typically brief delays in having his orders fulfilled gave Swann plenty of time to work up some bile.

This time he turned toward Tatum and snarled, "You lame-ass piece o' shit, gimme the goddamn whiskey already!"

Across the many miles they had covered, Tatum almost continuously spoke and chuckled—mainly to himself—about the success of their little ambush. He guffawed and whooped and clucked like a hen, basically entertaining himself the entire time, much to the irritation of his fellow riders. His head shook and bobbed like a puppy's and his knobby Adam's apple rose and fell with every yodeling laugh.

With the packhorse dallied to his saddle, he unofficially composed the supply train. During their first breather, he managed to dig the bottle of tangle-foot out of a sack. After a first round shared by all, he slipped it into his own saddlebag, within arm's reach; but before their journey was long under way, it seldom left his hands. It was apparent that he was making a hog of himself. His slurred speech showed it.

Swann rode single-mindedly in the lead, drawing Jessie's mount by a gut line and keeping up the pace. It was a hard, long trail ahead, and he didn't want to take it dry. He repeated his demand for the Overholt.

"I got it right here," Tatum said.

Swann slowed his pace and took the bottle when Tatum came up alongside.

"Hellfire, you weren't too in'erested in it before!" Tatum complained. "What's the goll'dang hullabaloo now—"

Before he knew what hit him, he lay on the dried-up bunchgrass, with a dizzying pain in his head. Swann towered above him, in his saddle.

"You bad-mouth me, boy, I'll shut your trap once and for all," he grumbled.

He uncorked the Overholt and held it up. It was only one-third full. "We got another full day's ride ahead of us," he said with cold, squinting eyes. "I won't tolerate no piss-eyed cowboy falling off his saddle every half-mile. You wanna git paid, you ride like you was a soldier; you wanna live, you best not cross C. J. Swann."

The shock that gripped Jessie since seeing Ki killed suddenly altered. *Another day! I'll probably be dead by nightfall tomorrow!*

The ridges of crumbling white rock that had loomed in the distance for so long now topped a series of scrub-carpeted slopes, lifting the trail toward the sky. The hills beyond turned dark as the sun fell behind them, causing the sky to glow a brilliant gunmetal gray while the land before them became like thick black velvet. The last fitful gusts of icy wind signaled sunset, and soon the air was still. Swann chose a level clearing for their bivouac.

Jessie feared the night more than any other time. With a little liquor and nothing better to occupy themselves with, killers like Swann could get uglier, meaner, and more low-down than a pit viper in a bedroll. When she dismounted, Tatum suggested they tie her arms and legs, which sparked a disagreement with Swann. Dupree settled things by tying her legs with a length of rope short enough to prevent her from running, but long enough for her to get around.

As Dupree knotted the rope above the mule ears of her boots, Jessie sensed what she thought was an apologetic shade to his expression. He was younger than she and very handsome. His short straight hair was black as jet; his body, lean and strong. His heavy woolen pants and sewn-on leather patches on the seat and inseam told her he earned his living in the saddle, and also that his living was meager. His well-worn John B., with its sweat-stained hatband and repaired stampede strap, had seen many a roundup and too little attention.

"That too tight?" he asked her, after bearing down on a knot.

Jessie shook her head, convinced that her senses were good. If she had anything like an ally in this losing game, Dupree was the one.

Watching her captors build a fire and rustle some grub would have been entertaining if Jessie hadn't been so famished. If their lives depended on living off the land, there was little hope for them. Tatum scorched his hands more than once and nearly doused the fire by spilling much of the pot's contents. The sludge he called beans could have been wet adobe, and the coffee was worse than the tonsil varnish they were drinking earlier. Dupree tore a small piece of hardtack in two and offered one to her. Reluctantly she ate it, desperate to keep up her strength in the bitter cold.

When time came for them to start bedding down, she asked, "Where do I sleep?"

Swann's low-pitched laugh sounded like a rusted chain pulley. "Where'd you like to sleep, honey?"

A chill shot through her. She didn't dare invite trouble and feared that anything she said would. Her silence elicited taunting snickers from Swann and Tatum. Dupree simply hung his head over a steaming tin of coffee. Their faces shimmered in the warm glow of the small fire. Finally Swann said, "Git her one o' them hides and set her up." He leaned over and lifted a bedroll. "Here," he said, throwing it to Jessie. "That's for you. See? We take good care of our guests." However, neither Dupree nor Tatum fetched the hide, since Swann didn't address either one of them. In an unexpected outburst he flung his coffee tin at them, yelling, "I said git the goddamn hide! Move!" Though the cup hit the ground harmlessly, the dregs of his coffee sprayed them both. Dupree jumped to his feet. His eyes flared with anger, which subsided quickly when he realized how little of the coffee had hit him.

"Sit down, kid," snarled Swann. "You be a good boy and just do as I say, and we'll git along just fine."

Tatum sniveled with evil glee and echoed Swann's words, earning a withering sneer from the scar-headed Boot Hill prophet. The skinny desperado fetched the hide and set it down upon Jessie before returning to his place beside the fire.

By noon next day the desperadoes had led Jessie into the far reaches of yesterday's horizon. The sparse shrubs and graveled earth gave away to carpeted valleys of brown grass dotted with small agaves and strewn with exposed white rock. On the ridges high above were stands of pine-fir, some of them naked of limbs on the side most assaulted by the relentless wind.

The trail hugged the shoulder of a steep slope and climbed.

Jessie realized they were following nothing more than a rocky path worn by wild animals—animals with much better footing than horses. The angle of the treeless slope became dizzying as the gully bottom fell farther away. Below, a trickling stream grew wider and faster as other creeks and springs fed it. Vegetation along the trail thinned until it almost vanished. To Jessie's worried concern, they started across a wide, loosely packed talus slope. Above them an immense, vertical wall of rock rose into the brooding sky, while the narrowing path twisted around increasingly numerous tumbledown rocks.

Tatum turned away and covered his eyes where the unbroken drop made him queasy. An occasional stone loosened from the trail's edge skittered over the talus until it splashed into the rushing stream below. Huge breakdown blocks, some the size of a Concord coach, littered the incline and even altered the flow of the stream. Jessie and Tatum breathed easier when the trail crested the slope and turned toward more level ground.

They passed through the cleavage between two bare, rounded slopes. Where the crease widened, they came in view of the mouth of a small, but spectacular, gorge. Through it ran a gushing stream that on the open side of the echoing chasm seemed to growl in the profound silence. Sluicing between high walls and jagged spires of rock, the small river turned sent up gusts of air that bit one's skin with its cold. A footbridge, dampened from the stream's white-water spray and less than ten yards long, carried the trail to the far side through a cleft in the canyon wall. "The cut," as Swann called it, was choked with trees and shrub, above which could be seen distant higher ground. The rocky trail through the cut followed the largest drainage gully of several that branched and wound through the dense bush between towering walls of rock. The bridge crossing was badly iced over. The party clopped across in single file toward the cut. Tatum cleared his nose and spat a thick gob into the flood.

"That sure was a right smart thing to do, C.J.," said Tatum, sometime later, "killin' that horse back there, and all. Ha! Even if them boys coulda rode themselves outta there, a kilt horse ain't no good to no one. I shoulda did the same dern thing."

"You didn't cuz you ain't got sense of a flea" was Swann's reply. Tatum just smiled and shook his head.

Then something cold touched his runny nose.

"Jumpin' Jehoshephat! That snow?" He held out his palms and looked at the sky. Something so simple, so common at higher altitudes, seemed difficult for him to comprehend. "Hey! It's snowin'!"

Swann looked up and mumbled, "Son of a bitch. Ain't that sompn."

"I hope it don't get any worse before we get there," Dupree added. He must have read Jessie's own thoughts.

But it did get worse.

Though not far from their destination they stopped for a meal beneath a copse of firs, not having eaten since morning. They huddled around the trunks with their buffalo hides bundled around them as the snow fell more heavily. Tatum played cookie again, volunteered by Swann with his usual tyrannical orders. None of the men seemed to mind the fact that Tatum was building a fire directly below a low branch of the tree that gave him shelter. It wasn't until Jessie spoke up that Tatum even took notice. The others remained silent, probably out of spite.

"I know what I'm doin'," he pouted. "I ain't standin' out in the snow just to feed your ugly faces."

The meal, like every other one they had so far, consisted of beans, bread, and coffee. No one ever asked for a second helping. Tatum got through cooking it well enough, never noticing that the hanging branch above the fire was dancing as if in a breeze. When it burst into flame, Tatum yelped like a stuck pig and leaped from underneath. Dupree found a downed length of tree limb. Swinging it like an ax, he snapped the burning branch off in three swipes and kicked it into the campfire. He glanced accusingly at Tatum. Swann, looking on, snickered, "Shit for brains."

After killing the fire, Tatum lodged his complaint. "I think Dupree should cook tomorrow. I'm tarred o' this shit. I didn't wanna cook in the first place. Only fair for somebody to do it some."

Exhausted, Jessie sat watching the snow fall as Tatum's futile whining trailed off. She was feeling terrifyingly isolated, desperately vulnerable. Losing Ki shook her confidence and still seemed unreal to her. Nonetheless, her shock didn't allow her to accept it or to grieve. While she couldn't deny what she saw, her heart would not give in. She was beyond help and knew it. Defenseless against the whims of three desperadoes, there seemed no way out; but one thought kept hope burning hotly: since these drygulching varmints hadn't killed her yet, there was always the possibility of escape. Perhaps killing her was not even part of their plan.

That, she swore, would be their worst mistake.

Within her darkened cell, curtained off for the night, Leslie Sykes was awakened by voices, the noise of keys and door locks, and approaching footsteps. A wave of fear swept through her as nightmares too believable to be dismissed lingered before her eyes. She heard the sound of two men, not the mob she had dreamed of, and they came asking questions, not accusing and condemning.

"Miss Sykes!"

It was Barefoot. He tapped on the bars with his key ring. "Forgive me, Miss Sykes. Someone's here to talk with you."

"One moment," she replied, gathering a woolen shawl around her as she sat up on her cot. "All right, Mister Barefoot. You may open the curtain."

In the shadow of Barefoot's candle stood the almond-eyed man she had missed since their only meeting. Immediately she recognized the fatigue and stress in Ki's face. As Barefoot stepped aside, Leslie's heart pounded at the sight of blood on Ki's clothing.

"What is it? What's wrong?"

"I need to speak with you," Ki said.

" 'Scuse me, ma'am," Barefoot interjected, "but this man's wounded and needin' attention. I think I've got—"

"Bring me clear water and bandaging, Marshal," Leslie ordered. "If you keep any iodoform in this palace, bring that as well." Barefoot hesitated, but Miss Sykes insisted. She shooed him off, but not before putting him to task. "Marshal! Please open the door for my guest first . . . if you please."

" 'Course, ma'am," he said, jangling keys. "And that's *deputy* marshal, ma'am."

"Yes, I know," she answered, "duly appointed," and off he went.

Stepping into her cell, Ki announced, "Miss Sykes, my employer, Jessica Starbuck, has been abducted. . . ."

Leslie sat him down on her cot and told him to remove his coat. "What happened to you?" she asked.

Ki produced a bent *shuriken* from his vest pocket and showed her the bullet hole through his coat, eliciting a gasp from the woman. She noticed the handsome lacquered sheath nested in the waistband of his trousers. Being a cultured woman, she recognized it as Japanese lacquer, although she had no knowledge of the foot-long blade it concealed, Ki's *tanto*.

"They killed my *shuriken*," he said with a poker face. "Ruined three of 'em—damn good ones, too."

As he told the story she sat beside him and undid his shirt to expose the wound. She could see it was superficial despite the enormous bruise already showing. Barefoot came with a basin of warm water and clean fabric. He told her he could find no iodoform.

"Bring some from Doctor MacNaughton, but tell him to stay home; I've been a nurse. No need to fetch him out in this cold." Turning to Ki as Barefoot left, she said, "I'm pleased you can be so stoic about this, but what about your friend?"

Ki sighed deeply. "Not sure. They killed one man, tried to kill another and me. They might do anything."

"And you think this is related to me and Vargas."

"Isn't it?"

"Undoubtedly. What else do you want to know?"

"You seem to know all about the Vargas family. Where would they bring her?"

She shrugged, wrung out a cloth in the water basin, and began cleaning the wound. "The Vargas family is like a separate state—a separate country, really. They control a large number of people over a vast area."

"I know that, but where would they take Jessie?"

She shook her head. "Your guess is as good as mine. Vargas controls land all the way from the Guadalupes to the Chisos. He's leased pasture to Fort Davis and Fort Quitman, hill country to Silver Star Mining . . . you name it. Practically from here to beyond the Sierra Diablo Mountains, it's Vargas country. They could have taken her anywhere."

She washed him slowly, resting her warm hands on his muscular stomach and shoulders, sensing the power he possessed. As she reached for the basin her shawl slipped away from the bodice of her cotton nightgown, offering Ki an unavoidable, splendid view of her luscious charms.

"What do you plan to do?" she asked while drying him.

"Ride out in the morning; track 'em down." Staring longingly at her large breasts swaying against the loose-fitting cotton, he could see everything but her nipples.

She said, "Bet you can't wait to get your hands on them," then looked up to catch his eyes staring down her nightgown. "On the kidnappers, that is."

Ki's smile widened slowly, slyly.

She said, "Did I catch your eyes peering where polite men shouldn't?"

"I wouldn't presume to insult you," he responded.

She gazed into his eyes a moment, then: "No insult taken. In fact, I'm flattered. I'm just glad you're not *that* kind of polite man." One hand rested on Ki's chest. She moved it across his nipple and lightly clenched it between two fingers. "So when will you be riding out?" she asked.

"Morning. Still have to round up some men to ride with me."

Her eyes fell. Her face darkened.

"I told you once that I am a doer," she said. "I also said that I have dreams. I've had some nightmares while I've been . . . 'residing' here, but . . ." She rested one hand on Ki's thigh. "I've dreamed some nice dreams of you, too." She looked into the silent man's eyes. "Do you find me attractive, Ki?"

"More than I can say."

She shifted herself, so that Ki caught an arousing glimpse of her smooth, slender legs, bare below the calf. She stood and went to the cell door where she reached for the hook holding the curtain opened.

"I would be terribly hurt if you were to ride out tomorrow morning and never come back, Ki. Life— my life, anyway—is too precarious to allow quality people and quality moments to slip through my fingers without trying to hold them, even just for a moment."

The soft candlelight shining through her sheer cotton gown was sufficient to show the furry tuft of pubic hair filling the crotch of her legs above delicately curved thighs.

"I can see your dedication to Miss Starbuck. It's admirable." She dropped the curtain and turned. Her pubic mound bulged through the front of the cloth. She sat beside him again.

"Do you love Jessica Starbuck?"

Ki wondered if Leslie could hear his heart pounding, could feel the heat coursing down his limbs and flushing his face, could smell the blood in his nose. He couldn't remember anyone ever asking him that question before, and his body screamed the answer, but who was he to even consider such a question? Half Japanese, half Caucasian, the offspring of a highborn woman whose position in society was ruined by her union with an unknown American businessman, Ki was an outcast in both cultures. The Starbuck family had given him a home, a mission in life, and a lifelong friend in Jessie, whose feminine softness perfectly complimented his masculine hardness. His respect, admiration, and dedication to her were limitless. But love?

"I'm only her foreman. It's not proper to ask that."

Whether he was Jessie's foreman or bodyguard was less important than the telling look in Ki's eyes.

"So," Leslie said with a sigh. "Here we are: two folks who may very well be dead within the next day or two, alone together in an elegant private suite, half dressed."

"Or half naked, if you're an optimist."

She laughed. "You know, Ki, I dreamed of a very fitting conclusion to such a scenario."

"Oh, really?"

She giggled again, lightly. "I love a decent man."

She kissed him on the lips softly, to which Ki responded with another, longer kiss that increased in passion. Their tongues met and explored. They parted and looked closely at each other. When their mouths met again, it was a release of every tension and pent-up emotion. Leslie's soft palms glided over Ki's chest until she found his hand, which she placed surely upon her own pendulous breast. His gentle teasing of her nipple drew moans of pleasure.

Ki whispered in her ear, "Barefoot's gonna be back any minute."

"He'll have to find his own fun," she said.

Her hand touched the sheath of the *tanto*. She slid her hand over its hard, smooth surface, ran her fingers along its length, then drew it from his waist and set it aside. She unbuttoned his trousers. Kissing him deeply, she slipped her hand down his taut stomach to find his stiffening flesh striving to stand free. She drew her warm palm along its length, drawing up his heavy scrotum, then grasping his erection by the root and squeezing it firmly.

Ki groaned for more, and Leslie went down with her thick, wet lips opened wide. She sucked his entire manhood deep into her mouth until his engorged cock was glistening wet. She paused and lifted her gown, gasping, "Quickly, put it in!" In one move she straddled his legs, with her back and soft pale ass facing him. She spread herself wide and came down slowly, taking in every last inch of his thick, veined shaft, making even his pubic hair disappear beneath the delicate crease of her butt. She rose and fell smoothly and quickened the pace. Ki's legs went taut with concentrated erotic energy.

He held her by her hips, his fingers dimpling her soft, shiny flesh. Her butt cheeks jiggled and bounced with each clapping contact. Arching her back slightly, she rocked forward and back, wriggled in circles, and flexed her vaginal muscles, the stimulation becoming unbearably intense for her wildly bucking partner.

She kept her gown bunched above her waist with one hand. With the other she stroked Ki's balls and ran her fingertips lightly over the sensitive creases and short hairs around them. She heard his breathing turn heavier, felt him thrust more urgently. She quickened her pace again. By now his cock was drenched with her flowing juices. As his climax overtook him like the onrush of a storm, she released her gown, planted her hand flat on Ki's stomach for support, and clenched her hungry love canal tightly until she drew every bit of his heaving ejaculations out of him. He broke out in a flowing sweat and pushed and pulled her pelvis across himself, grinding out his last bolts of passion. When his thrusting subsided, she relaxed upon his slowly fading hard-on and screwed him gently until they heard Barefoot's boots on the boardwalk outside.

She wiped the perspiration from her forehead and pinned back the curtain while Ki closed his trousers and threw on a shirt.

"I'm sorry I can't help you find your friend," she whispered breathlessly. "But I want you to know that I hope she's all right, sincerely. And I hope I'll see you again."

Barefoot came thundering in. "Got the iodoform!" Invited inside, the deputy took a look at Ki's wound and said, "Land sakes, ma'am, that's some cleaning you done gave him, all over like. Looks like he got himself some real bad sun, too."

"It pays to be thorough," she said with a smirk.

Early next morning Ki and the deputy went from door to door raising a posse. They went first to the homes of men who were part of the town's Public Safety Committee. Each man who came out searched for another in turn. Folks began gathering before the marshal's office as word spread across town. Four men on horseback arrived ready to ride, patiently awaiting instructions from Ki and the lawdog. Barefoot asked Ki to arrange for supplies from Whittaker's store while he ran an errand. Two men leading their mounts by the reins approached Ki.

"We'd like to ride with y'all," said the tall one, a barrel-chested redhead with freckles. He extended his hand. "Name's Joe Dell Branch. My friends call me J.D."

"Are you with the committee?" Ki asked.

"No, sir. We just heard what happened. Wanna do our part. This here's Wade McClung. A good man, quick with a six-shooter. The best there is."

McClung was a short guy about Ki's age—around thirty—with scraggly blond hair the texture of straw. He nodded toward Ki with a low-voiced "Howdy." Taking note that their rigs looked like rental gear, Ki thanked them and asked them to wait by their mounts.

In a short while, Boyd returned. The passel of bystanders watched as the eleven men geared up to leave. Mr. Stewart provided two packhorses burdened with plenty of food, ammunition, and additional bedding. Barefoot judged it would be a long trail by Ki's description of the country.

"Where'd you go?" Ki asked him.

"Went to see Vargas. He's lodging at a house down by the creek. I just had to ask him if he had a notion where Jessie done gone."

"What he say?" Ki asked.

"Nothin' I didn't expect. I just told him she was missing, and he said, 'Who knows what kinds of banditos are out there?' No feeling in that boy, not even for a woman. Couldn't care less." He clicked his tongue. "I plumb don't trust him."

A kid came galloping down the street on a dark-spotted dapple, Appaloosa-bred. He reined in at the hitching rail and, leaping from the saddle, approached Barefoot.

"I'm riding with you men." His cheeks were ruddy, his eyes fired up. He couldn't have been more than seventeen.

Barefoot said, "Your momma know you done gone?"

"Ain't nothing she can say to keep me," he said with tight lips.

"Sure, you wanna go bad, but it wouldn't be right. No telling what might happen, who might get hurt. It would break your mama's heart if . . ." He couldn't put words to the thought, but realized the kid wouldn't be dissuaded. All Barefoot could do was nod reluctantly and tell the kid to saddle up. He turned to Ki and said, "Ain't no way somebody's gonna stop him from following, so he might as well ride. Sam Judd. Howie's brother."

★

Chapter 7

Jessie snuggled deeper into the soft pillow, pulled the blanket high over her head, and sighed. It was heaven to sleep in her own bed again after such a long journey. The ranch was as quiet as on a Sunday morning. She could have stayed there all day long and not moved a muscle—had she not remembered where she really was.

With a start she raised her head. The pillow was musty, but she really was in bed, a wooden cot actually, on a lumpy, thin cotton mattress. She thrust her hand beneath the pillow and was relieved to find her saddlebag still where she put it. She faced a stone wall, and the air outside her covers was warm. She was in the cabin. Slivers of light piercing the wall planks above the stone told her it was morning. She had slept since they first arrived, probably fourteen hours or more. Still the wind roared down the mountain. A night and the better part of two days in the open left her bushed, and nothing short of a hungry bear would have kept her awake.

She stretched and rolled over. Her ankles were still

tethered just inches apart. Her eyes opened and, to her misfortune, met Swann's. He was sitting against the opposite wall on one of the two cots there, tapping his boot with a piece of kindling. His lurid smile sickened her, and she turned away.

"You sleep just like a baby, don't you?" he taunted. "And a mighty cute one, too."

It was an old cabin, built into the side of a hill on a low stone wall, probably a shelter for outriders or miners. She looked around for her first take of the place in daylight. Firewood and cow chips had been stockpiled inside and out. Shelves along the back wall were lined with tins of Arbuckle's coffee, flour, oats, a few metal plates, cups, and pots, and these men's favorite food, dried beans. There was one tiny window on the downhill side. A small potbellied cook stove stood across from a pile of wood next to her cot and kept the place tolerably warm. At her feet a fourth cot lined the wall. A small square table with three backless stools filled the middle of the floor. They were the only other furniture, all of it scarred and carved with men's initials and graffiti.

Blinding whiteness filled the room, followed by a wave of frigid air, as Dupree entered. He carried a pot full of snow, which he placed on the stove to melt for drinking water. He observed Jessie carefully without a word, just the slightest nod possible. He removed his coat, pulled a stool close to the stove, and sat leaning against the wall. Nothing was said, and there was nothing to do. *This is going to be a hellish long stay,* Jessie thought, *no matter how short.*

Dupree turned up two things from a sack Swann had packed: a deck of playing cards and a slab of bacon. The sight of them was like fleas in Tatum's trousers. Tatum was angered that he didn't know about the bacon soon-er—on the trail, when good food was all he dreamed about. He also fancied himself a pretty handy poker player and relished the notion of cutting the deck some. After Dupree had lost half a dozen games of solitaire, Tatum challenged him.

"With what money?" Dupree said.

"You don't have none, either, so I'll take your mark," Tatum snorted. "And we can use bullets for chips. C'mon." Dupree gave in, looking depressed. During the game, Tatum finished off the dregs of the Overholt and nervously tapped the empty bottle with a cartridge.

"See if it stopped snowing yet," Swann growled. Dupree and Tatum looked at each other.

"I do the cookin'," Tatum grumbled. "I think he means you."

"I hauled all that firewood," Dupree answered, casting a thumb over his shoulder, "and you're closer to the door."

Neither of them moved a muscle except for Tatum's continued tapping of the glass bottle in his characteristically spastic rhythm. With some discomfort he said, "I ain't never seen it snow like this before." It went quiet, but for the wind.

"One o' you horse cocks gonna look outside before winter's over?" Swann roared. His eyes were wild and bloodshot. Tatum flitted a glance at Dupree, who finally gave in. He slapped his hand on the table and kicked out his stool.

Stomping to the door, he said, "I'll tell you right now, Caddo Jack: this'll be the last time I play fetch for you." He opened and closed the door, softly saying, "Still snowing," then turned and said, "I ain't your woman, and I ain't your dog. I'm here to do a job, not wipe your sorry ass halfway across the state. Next time you do it yourself. Or get cookie to do it."

Tatum slammed the table with the cartridge, and Swann whistled at the threatening language.

"Ooo-wee! Ain't we tough," he exclaimed. "And what you fixin' to do if I want my ass wiped only by you? Huh, tough guy?" Dupree remained silent and sat down again, leaving Swann laughing to himself. The scar-headed irritant mumbled, "Yeah, I thought so."

"Play cards," Dupree said to Tatum, "and stifle it," before he could reply.

Jessie dozed after that, and she was unsure of how

75

much time had passed when she awoke. The light in the window had dimmed. It must have been near dusk. The poker game continued, Dupree owning an arsenal of cartridge chips. Still Tatum persisted in tapping the empty bottle. His winnings wouldn't have loaded a six-shooter.

Dupree kept a running tally of each of their winnings. Tatum, being unable to read or write and being cocksure he would humiliate his opponent, magnanimously encouraged Dupree to keep the tab; but as the game consistently turned against him he pouted and refused to cooperate. He began to show suspicion about what Dupree recorded.

They occasionally played seven-card stud as a change-up from five-card draw. Before the first deal of each new game Dupree insisted that Tatum sign a mark for his debt. Unless Tatum complied, Dupree refused to play anymore, denying Tatum the chance to win back his losses. Tatum became belligerent.

"What in hell good is it to give you my mark iff'n I ain't got no money?"

"Okay," Dupree answered, "then I'll take it out of your share of what Vargas is paying us. All right? Here, I'll write down like this, 'Vargas . . . owes Dupree . . . from . . . Tatum's share.' There. You must put your mark on it, and I'll get my money direct from Vargas."

Tatum grumblingly made his mark, demanding a sum total of his losses each time despite having little idea of how badly he was eroding the money he expected to earn from Vargas. Each successive hand he lost was followed by a worsening argument—where did Dupree get that queen? How did that ten of spades turn up again? Where did Dupree learn to shuffle? Then the infernal tapping would resume.

Swann couldn't take it any longer. With an unintelligible curse he pitched a tin of coffee at the offender, shattering the bottle on the table and peppering him with a spray of jagged shards. The coffee tin flew open, broadcasting a shower of brown grinds across half the

76

room and stinging Tatum's eyes and face. The skinny man fell backwards off his stool and sprang up again just as quickly, stamping his feet and reeling around the room with his hands to his face, bouncing off things he couldn't knock over. Dupree leaped to his feet, and Jessie expected a brawl. Swann surprised them all by bursting into gales of hysterics that sounded as much like tubercular coughing as laughter.

"What in hell you laughing at?" Tatum shrieked. "I can't see a damn thing!"

Dupree found a pail of cool water and guided Tatum's hands to it. The agonized fellow splashed himself repeatedly and lifted his eyelids to free the grains stuck underneath. Tiny red pricks showed up on his face and neck where the glass had needled him. His eyes turned beet-red and nearly closed entirely. In his whimpering, whining voice he pouted, "You dumb ass, Ceej! You're as dumb as they come, I swear," whereupon Swann's laughing suddenly and eerily ceased.

"Watch what you say," he warned. "I was just having some fun with you, but don't you ever cuss me. Y'hear? You just watch what you say."

Tatum was shaken by the low tone of his voice. He said, "I wasn't cussin' you, Ceej. I was just . . . I couldn't see, and my eyes was burning fierce. I wasn't cussin' you."

Swann nodded, as if to say, *You'd better not,* and relaxed again, returned to doing nothing. Jessie couldn't believe her eyes. She thought, *At this rate, these snakes'll kill each other—if I'm lucky.*

Night came early. The snow had stopped falling a few hours earlier, with less than half a foot accumulated on open ground. Except for the sound of forks scraping beans off metal plates, the cabin was quiet enough to hear the wood settling in the stove. Jessie had to ask to go outside to relieve herself. Swann eyed her evilly from the table, where he stirred sugar into his muddy coffee. He told Dupree to keep an eye on her, to which Dupree replied, "Where the hell is she going in this weather? She'd die out there if she tried anything," but he put his coat on anyway.

When Jessie threw off her buffalo hide, Swann smirked, his eyes twinkled. "You sure are one fine piece . . . Imagine, if it weren't for that skinflint Vargas, I never woulda met you."

Tatum tittered. Jessie's ears burned with the mention of Vargas's name. As for Swann, he scared her down to her toes, but she preferred dying while giving him hell than to ever let him get the best of her. She bunched the hide over her pillow, where the saddlebags lay out of sight.

There wasn't much chance for privacy outside, but Dupree proved to be humane about it. He promised to stay by the door while she took care of herself behind the building. He encouraged her not to do anything rash; he had no violent intentions, but the others had already shown their true colors. Jessie believed him, for what it was worth.

Back inside, Tatum handed her a plate of sludge he called dinner. She turned it away, as hungry as she was.

"I think I just disposed of your last specialty," she said, and headed for her cot.

The others laughed; Tatum threw a hissy. He refused to cook anymore and challenged Jessie to do better, with what they had. Dupree accused him of taking everything too seriously; after all, he and Swann were eating the stuff. Swann, however, liked Tatum's idea.

"It's a woman's job anyway," Swann decreed. "Tomorrow, you cook, Miss Snooty. I like my food touched by feminine hands." A thought occurred to him that made him pause. "That's why I had Tatum do the cooking in the first place!"

Tatum slammed Jessie's plate to the floor, cursed aloud, and fell on his cot to stare at the rough-beamed ceiling.

It snowed again late that night. Wind moaned across the cabin's rickety eaves and drove icy pellets against the walls and window with an insistent pattering. Jessie slept deeply despite the men's snoring. The unfamiliar sounds of the old building—the creaks and snaps and taps—were becoming memorized and dismissed, even though footsteps across the old floor were easily mistaken for them. In her deep sleep Jessie's wakeful subconscious didn't notice that the floor creaked when the wind was still, that something tapped near the stove when no wood had settled.

She lay on her back, with the buffalo hide pulled up to her chin and the woolen blanket beneath wrapped around her head. Her breath turned to vapor, which vanished in the unlit room. She had a dream of falling, which woke her.

The ominous shadow of a man loomed over her. Her dream had been sparked by his nudging the cot with his leg as he reached for her covers. Before she was fully awake, the covers were lifted. Cold air rushed across her hands that lay folded across her belt buckle. She cringed.

It was Swann.

She flattened herself against the wall, causing her cot to creak loudly. Her eyes bulged, straining to see. She could barely make out his face, but the hideous wrinkled scar that was his scalp was unmistakable. There was a glint of gold from the small crucifix that still dangled from his neck. His chilling, thick chuckle bubbled from his chest like sulphurous air bubbling up through fouled mud.

"Don't come any closer," Jessie warned. Dupree's cot creaked and snapped. Glancing over his shoulder, Swann must have realized Dupree was awake and watching. He turned back to Jessie with a harrumph.

"Just looking," he growled, dropped the blankets, and returned to his bed.

The smell of bacon next morning practically pulled Tatum out of his bedroll by the nostrils. With Dupree's help fetching snow for water and keeping the stove hot, she worked up a decent meal that included fresh-made biscuits and boiled oats flavored with bacon grease. In fact, keeping her rude hosts in mind, Jessie flavored everything except her own food with bacon grease, and lots of it—in the coffee, in the biscuit batter—and she figured correctly that these poor slobs were too hard up to know the difference. It placed cooking for these ingrates in a more attractive light. They might think it was high cuisine. They also might miss the fact that within a day or so, they'd be hard put not to shit their drawers involuntarily with that much grease in their diet. As they glutted themselves on the unsavory foods they mistook her prankster's grin for the proud smile of a caring, motherly woman.

"I need to wash."

It had taken Jessie all day to work up the courage to say it. After last night she felt Dupree's presence might be enough to check Swann's high-handed outlawry, so she said it, and also demanded their assurances that she would have her privacy and that she would go unmolested. Her demands elicited more sneering gibes from the foul-tempered hoot owl. The idea of bowing to the wishes of a mere woman, especially one reduced to a captive, offended him.

"You cin wash that pretty little butt o' yours right here in front of us. I kin use some diversion."

"I want you and the others to wait outside," she insisted. "It's not snowing, and it won't take long."

Dupree admired her. She was gutsy, maybe too gutsy, but she stood her ground in the name of dignity. That was something he could only vaguely recall in his own life. It was as if Jessie had opened a barn-sized door to his heart, only to reveal a gaping void where there was once humanity.

"Let her wash in private," he said. "It won't kill us to wait outside a few minutes. Besides, the horses need to be checked and fed. C'mon, C.J., don't be so hard on her."

As he spoke, Tatum looked on quietly, then donned his coat and hat. He gulped down some of Jessie's coffee and walked out. Swann hissed in disbelief and scuffed his heels toward the door.

"I'll leave you two girls alone together," he scoffed.

Dupree stepped outside a minute later and planted

himself like a sentry in front of the door. Tatum was puffing on a roll of tobacco, leaning against the cabin, peering into the window periodically in hope of sighting something he hadn't seen in a dog's life. Dupree suggested he take a walk.

When Swann swaggered in again after Jessie was done, she thanked him. His crooked smile looked forced and angry. She was glad to see Dupree enter next.

Swann leered and said, "So y'all fresh and lovely again, sweetie?" Jessie ignored him. He lifted a sack from under his cot and withdrew from it a full bottle of home-brewed rotgut. The squeak and pop of the cork drew Tatum like a fly to shit. He looked about to die when he saw Swann lean back for a long, deep swig that appeared downright painful.

"Where'd that come from?" Tatum asked.

Swann hissed, "Outta my bag," at which Tatum rushed to the shelf and retrieved a cup. He held it out to Swann like a begging poodle. "Get outta my sight," Swann muttered. Tatum stood dejected, looking to Dupree as if for help.

"C'mon, Ceej, how about it?" Tatum coaxed. "I shared mine with you. . . ."

"That's because you're a sniveling weakling and a coward. You had no choice." Swann plopped onto his cot, with his bottle of coffin opener at his side, and began drinking heartily, leering all the while at Jessie as she prepared another pot of java.

"You nice and clean down below now, lady?" Swann jeered. The firewater was stoking him up more with each swallow. "I think you should show us what a fine job you did washing them secret places. How 'bout it? Let's see how much cleaner you are than us low-down skunks. C'mon. What do you say?"

Jessie lay beneath the covers and faced the stone wall.

Dupree said, "Lay off, C.J."

Swann snarled back, "You and her kin have your little gabfest when I'm done. You cin make all the girl talk you want. I just think it's a damn shame this pretty little wench is with us all this time, soakin' up our hospitality, eatin' our food, tellin' us when to leave the goddamn cabin, and what do we get? Nothin'! Not real friendly-like, is it? I think I might be inclined to work out a trade here. How about this. How about we keep on feeding you, and you let us in on that hot little secret you keep tucked so tight between your legs."

Dupree slapped the table hard enough to make the plates jump. "Damn it, Swann, you're going too far," he shouted. "We're here to do a job, and I want to see it go right. Not like last time."

Swann snapped, "Don't you badmouth me about that, boy!"

"Just lay off the girl. You said this was gonna be easy; nobody's supposed to get hurt. You already killed two men, and the marshal's probably after us already. Don't mess this up any more than it is."

Swann's chest seemed to swell as he gathered himself to react to Dupree's mutiny. His eyes flared like a demon's, but before he got a word out, Tatum spoke up.

"Dupree's right, Ceej. Leave the girl be."

Jessie's ears perked up in the profound and tense silence. They were all waiting for something, and it was Swann's turn. The lines were drawn, and it would get ugly if Swann were faced with backing down. Dupree sensed that. Remembering what little he knew about Swann's involvement with Vargas, he tried to defuse the powder keg.

"You realize she's your only weapon against Vargas, you know." His pause let that thought sink into Swann's thick-scarred skull and gave Dupree some time to improvise. "Seems to me Vargas wants her kept safe because he wants her to himself. Didn't you say she's some kind of big landowner? Well, so is Vargas. He needs her for something; I don't know what. But if you got her, and something happens to her, you'll be fighting with an unloaded gun against Vargas and all his *pistoleros*."

"You take me for some kind of fool?" Swann said in

a choked voice. "I know what I got here, and I see the way you stiff-pricked coyotes been eyeing her." He took another jolt from his bottle and wiped his his dripping chin with his sleeve. "You two just stay clear of her. She's mine, and when the time is right, I'll do whatever the hell I want with her."

Everyone in the room heard a liquid rumbling come from Swann's abdomen. A few moments later he slammed down the bottle and put on his coat. He pointed his finger at Tatum as he hurried out.

"I gotta shit. You touch that bottle while I'm gone, I'll blow a hole clear through you."

The door slammed, and Jessie heard his feet scrunching through the deep snow away from the cabin.

"Thanks," she said softly. "Both of you." Dupree took a seat without acknowledging her, and Tatum reclined on his cot. She asked, "What makes a man so ornery?"

Dupree sniffed. "C.J. Swann sure is that."

Jessie said, "You once called him Caddo Jack. What's that about?"

Dupree got up to pour himself a cup of warm coffee. He sat down and thought a moment. Swann made an interesting, if horrifying, portrait, if anyone cared to paint it. Dupree attempted to do so in broad strokes.

"Bluecoats nicknamed him that a long time ago," he began, "as I heard it, 'cause he's a half-breed. His mother was a farmer's wife from East Texas. She was kidnapped by Caddos—back in the forties, I think. They sold her to Comanches, and she got to liking that life, I guess, so she stayed on with 'em, had a son. That was all before the war.

"Now, C.J.'s always been the surviving type, but he was always more Indian than Christian. So when the Rebs came through, he played Comanche if the Comanches happened to be raiding the bluecoats that month. When the bluecoats came through, he played Caddo along with all the other Caddos who scouted for them. But the Kiowa didn't much care for Caddo army scouts and neither did the Rebs, and one or the other nearly ended his story before it was barely something to tell, more times than once. Had himself a few run-ins with Kiowa, and he says he's killed more of them with his bare hands than he could count. Some Indians thought he was white; whites thought he was Indian. He's like a hare that changes coat every season. Trouble was, during the war, there were only so many coats a man could wear. So he caught some hell, 'specially from them Union boys."

"Is that how he came to look the way he does?"

"You mean the head? Naw!" A wry smile wrinkled Dupree's handsome face and revealed his single dimple. "Ugly son of a bitch, ain't he? Naw, that happened, oh, eight, nine years ago, Staked Plains . . . C.J.'s real touchy about it, too. He was a skinner for some buffalo runners up that way. Seems they were ambushed by a band of Comanches—his own people, really. A bunch of the hunters were killed; the others high-tailed for their lives. C.J. took a fall. Next thing he knows, he's getting a mighty close shave." His laughter punctuated the story once again. "What really got his goat was, it seems the Comanche lifting his scalp was a goddamn squaw! No wonder he gets ill when folks find out!"

"But why only half his head? What happened?" Jessie pressed. The smile vanished from the handsome scoundrel's face, and he cast his eyes down.

"He murdered the woman before she could finish it."

The door burst open. Swann stormed in, growling about the cold. His teeth were chattering as he stepped up to the stove to warm himself.

"Not bad enough I'm blowin' mud outta my ass, I gotta freeze my pizzle off besides. Hey, you got something hot to drink around here?"

Jessie stood and went for the coffeepot on the stove. "Right here in front of you," she said, swirling it to blend the bacon grease before pouring. "Here's a great big hot cup. Drink up."

For the first time since Jessie started cooking, loss of appetite became an issue that evening. Swann's abdominal cramps had barely eased all day long, while

Dupree denied his discomfort out of sheer politeness. Nonetheless, Jessie didn't fail to notice the few urgent exits he made and his prolonged absences spent in the cold. If she hadn't felt so endangered by the men's violent whims, she would have laughed out loud. Only Tatum seemed immune to Jessie's laxative recipes. He appeared to her to be enjoying the first regular meals in his life. He was even enthusiastic about his next, so Jessie put him to work hauling wood and stoking the fire.

Getting around even the small space in the cabin was a frustrating affair. The rope still binding her legs allowed only the shortest steps, and she was forced to shuffle everywhere she went. It was particularly burdensome in the snow, which averaged nearly a foot deep in the open. Every trip outdoors soaked her ankles in freezing meltwater and entailed drying her pant legs and boots by the stove afterward. She was getting tired of it.

Afraid to address Swann directly, if only because it would acknowledge his position of authority, she stood, quiet and still, before them all until she drew their attention. Then she said, "You know I can't run from you. There's no place to go. I need to have this rope removed so I can get around better, do the cooking and the chores."

"And steal one of the horses, too," Swann rasped. Tatum paused momentarily from stacking wood, but said nothing.

"I wouldn't get far. It would be suicide," she replied.

When no one responded, Dupree took a knife from the table. He knelt on one knee and, without looking at Swann, cut the rope from both ankles. His eyes, just inches from her crotch, cast over Jessie's entire body in a manner that hinted of shyness. Or maybe apology.

Tatum said to Jessie, "Stove's all set," and he sat back on Jessie's cot. "And there's plenty of wood for the night."

Jessie became nervous seeing Tatum resting there. He held a wide piece of bark and was snapping pieces from it, throwing them at the stovepipe. When struck just right it gave a dull *kung* sound. Jessie mixed batter at the table, trying not to appear anxious. One sheet of bark spent, Tatum leaned down for another, placing one hand on the mattress inches from the pillow. He used the iron poker to pull the chunk closer. His movement pulled the buffalo hide down, uncovering most of the pillow. He sat up again and resumed pitching pieces.

"Tatum, would you mind getting the tin of flour from the shelf for me?" she asked, but before he reacted, Dupree got up from his stool saying, "I'll get it." Jessie was miffed by the sudden dutiful responses she was getting from these two normally uncooperative men.

There was the squeak and pop of a cork behind her. Swann took a mouthful of liquor and sloshed it around his mouth, cheeks puffed out, before swallowing. He exhaled forcefully and shook his head in the aftermath.

"Sure is good to see a man who gets around a kitchen as good as you, Dupree," he scoffed. "That's what I like in a man—true grit and a holster full o' recipes." His snickering was replaced by the sound of his gullet sucking down more rotgut.

Jessie set the flour tin down and turned toward Tatum. Her heart skipped a beat. Leaning down for yet another chunk of bark, he was resting his free hand flat on the pillow. She froze at the sight of the pillow's edge lifting up to reveal the brown leather saddlebag beneath. She prayed she was the only one who noticed. Tatum sat up once more, and the pillow flattened out again. He saw nothing.

I've got to get this imbecile off there.

"Tatum, I'm making tortillas. Come look at these beans and tell me if they're the way you like them."

He tossed his last two pieces of bark and slowly leaned toward the pillow, saying, "Any old way's just fine. I like your cooking more better than mine."

"Who cares how he likes 'em?" Swann grouched. "I could shit in his plate and he'd think it was goddamn paté, for chrissakes."

Tatum sat bolt upright before making contact with the pillow. "You're gonna have to shit in somebody's plate awright, 'cause you done shit every place else around here. You smell like a walking outhouse!"

Swann laughed deeply at Tatum's childish return. He knew he smelled foul, but the more he drank, the less he cared. "You don't exactly smell like roses, friend. Y'all can sleep outside if it gets too thick." He laughed, stifling himself with the mouth of the bottle.

"I just might," Tatum said. He planted both hands on the mattress and pushed himself up and headed for the door. Jessie's heart relaxed. Before he rounded the table, Swann called to him.

"Here, you want a cup o' giggle-soup, Tatum? Catch." He threw a tin cup across the room. Tatum lurched for it and missed. It clinked against the stone wall above Jessie's cot and came to rest at the edge of her pillow.

Jessie and Tatum went for it simultaneously, but Tatum was closer. He picked it up and stalled, staring down at the mattress. He reached his other hand down and brushed it across smooth brown leather.

"Hey . . . What's your saddlebags doing here?" he said.

Jessie didn't know how far to go. She said, "I needed someplace to put my soiled clothes. Maybe you fellas will let me wash them soon. They're not smelling too fresh, I'm afraid."

Swann snickered, "That's when I like 'em best!"

Tatum lifted the bag. "Nice leather! Real nice." He went for the buckled strap. Jessie tried to talk gently, saying, "Please, I'd be very embarrassed if you saw them. It's my time of the month."

He hesitated. He dropped the cup and gave the bag a squeeze.

"I ain't never seen you change your clothes. You was wearing the same things after your wash."

He quickly undid the buckle, slipped in his hand, and pulled out a thick, folded sheaf of papers. As he riffled through them his eyes bulged at the sight of what surely looked like currency—the finely engraved patterning, the fancy lettering, the etched likenesses of proud bald eagles with wings spread wide, official-looking seals. Tatum couldn't read, but he recognized dollar signs and those egg-shaped symbols for large amounts of money—strings of zeros grouped in threes.

"Hey, Ceej! Look ahere! I ain't never seen no money like this before!"

★

Chapter 8

Barefoot stuck three fingers deep into the horse manure and lifted some to his nose. He sniffed. It had almost no odor until he crumbled it under his thumb and sniffed again. It was cold, but not frozen, and its color was still good.

"It's them, all right," he said, dropping it and wiping his hand on his denims. With the eye of a native tracker he had led the posse across the windswept savannah from where Jessie was taken, through barren badland, and into the hills to the west. The kidnappers had made no effort to conceal their trail, which made Sam Judd's innards bubble with anticipation. Quietly, confidently, Barefoot spoored the kidnappers' horses into rougher terrain.

The hoofprints were still crisp, their edges still sharp, despite the wind and flying debris. Leaves and twigs within the prints more often had been stepped on than blown into the prints, which meant the prints were made more recently than the debris had blown into them. In this weather, that had to be very recent.

Where the bush was dense and trampled or broken, he saw signs of at least five horses.

"They headed for high ground," he said, "and by the looks of that rainseed, they're getting snowed or rained on about now."

Sam Judd and the others peered to the ridges ahead, which, when not shrouded in low gray cloud, were dusted a deathly white.

They had ridden almost nonstop, eating in the saddle and forcing those who had to relieve themselves to catch up. At times the progress was painfully slow as Barefoot and one or two others proceeded on foot from sign to sign. They tried to make up lost time whenever the trail followed an animal path or squeezed around natural obstacles—whenever the choices were more obvious than the spoor. Barefoot guessed they were little more than half a day behind Jessie and her captors.

Their greatest disappointment was the realization that the route to their apparent destination would have been much shorter had it come directly out of Sarah. Because they had begun to track from the ambush point, their course described an immense triangle stretching many arduous miles and consuming precious hours. Their disappointment proved easier to swallow than the anxiety that seized them as the terrain buckled and rose.

With trepidation young Judd watched the stream they were following course its way down the gully as the trail continued to rise, shouldering the grassy slope. At the sight of the talus slope his feet and hands went cold. He rode near the rear of the line, a few places behind the two packhorses that were kept tethered to the horns of their lead horses.

"We gonna cross *that*?" he asked incredulously of no one in particular. "It's all loose rock!"

The rider ahead of him said over his shoulder, "If I knowed we was gon' foller this here wolfer-crost mountain lion trail in the snow, I'da stayed on home fer damn sure."

Their progress slowed drastically as the horses had more trouble placing their hooves. The trail was a thin ribbon of white snaking across a slope of mottled dark stone. The wind against their backs was all the blessing they could hope for.

"This is crazy!" said the man behind Sam Judd. "Ain't no sense killing ourselves. Folks we're tracking prob'ly dead already!"

Joe Dell Branch, the large redhead riding behind the packhorses, said, "Barely anything left of their hoofprints. What is this guy following, their *smell*?"

Near its highest reach the trail shrank to a worn space that was hardly level. Ki's horse slipped and nearly stumbled, recovering its footing just as Ki braced for a fall. A small patch of loosened earth gave way, shrinking that part of the trail further. The next two riders avoided the spot while the first of the men leading a packhorse kept a roving eye forward and behind. Holding the hitch taut, he turned to keep some uphill pressure on the packhorse's bridle when he felt his own mount slip out from under him. With the sickening rumble of rock grinding upon rock a length of trail nearly three horses long suddenly collapsed.

He and his mount were the first to be swallowed by the scouring landslide. The lead rope dragged the packhorse down with him, and the animal's kicking hooves loosened still more snow-covered rock. The rider nearly managed to save himself, reining his mount and digging his heels feverishly to regain the trail; but as the top-heavy pack horse tumbled, he knew he was a goner. As more stone fell away, the trail began to disappear toward the rear of the posse, and the next man back soon found himself in a heel-raking skid over jagged, toppling scree, irresistibly hauling several hundred pounds of packhorse and supplies on top of himself.

The terror-stricken neighing and screaming of horrified broomtails, the crack of splintered wood as the packsaddle disintegrated, and the resonant thunder of sliding earth chilled the spines of every rider who sat helplessly by. The first two horses to fall plummeted wildly, spreading supplies and material down the slope as packs and lashings tore apart. The second pair's hock-scarring descent became more tragic when the packhorse toppled and crashed upon the rider below. Already scrambling to quit his saddle, he was struck down sidelong and rolled as he fell. His foot became twisted within a tapadero, and he screamed in torture as he was stirrup-dragged over jagged scree toward the icy stream below.

The posse froze in terror as the collapse of stone and flesh continued, and the snow downhill turned red with blood. The rider just ahead of the collapse dismounted in a frantic effort to act but slipped in the snow and injured himself needlessly when he fell hard on his elbow. He sat cradling his arm as the deadly downrush erupted into the water.

The first rider to fall came out of his stirrups midway down and lay unconscious as the rubble settled around him. His horse came to a stop against a huge breakdown block, where it found its legs and stood in wildeyed terror upon the one surface that wouldn't give, rabbity and bloodied from chest to tail. The second packhorse lay still, with its head downhill. The other lead horse tried in vain to stand while its rider still had his foot in the stirrup. His anguished screaming echoed from above. When the animal tried again, the rider drew his pistol in desperation and sent a bullet through its brain, gasping curses as he fell back in agony. The fourth horse lay panting and broken, with its tail drifting in the stream water.

"Robbie! Ed!" shouted the men as they dismounted. Boyd and several others followed them downhill, carrying rope, while others tended the horses.

Ed, the conscious one, weakly called out Boyd's name. He seemed on the verge of tears. "I'm hurt real bad. Jesus, m' leg's all twisted up. I can't feel my toes!"

Two men reached Robbie and rolled him over gently. His face was caked with reddened snow. "He's breathing!" one of them shouted.

There were no poles with which to make stretchers or a travois, so blankets and canvas were sent down to roll into makeshift splints and slings. Ed's leg was twisted nearly backward from the pelvis, and he fell into a shocked faint when they tried to bind it. A body-sized sling was rigged for Robbie. Two men guided him as they climbed alongside, while Ki and another man hoisted him uphill.

Once the injured men were looked after, Sam Judd descended with a ground cloth into which he collected the scattered supplies. His thin leather gloves gave little protection from the cold, and his fingers began to stiffen. As he stooped to retrieve a bag of provisions, a gunshot shattered the relative calm, then another, making him flinch. He saw the two fallen horses kick spasmodically after the bullets struck, then go still.

The horse standing on the block was skittish and streaked with blood. It favored one foreleg. When the men finally managed to bring him down, he collapsed forward. The leg was stripped to the bone, apparently broken above the fetlock. Crestfallen, Barefoot ordered the animal stripped of its gear. He released the tie-down on his mare's leg and lifted out his pistol, a Smith & Wesson New Model No. 3 chambered for .44 rimfire. He cocked it sadly and put down the wounded broomtail after a long, apologetic stare.

The man who cracked his elbow was shivering like a leaf in the wind. He was able to walk well enough, but riding would be tough. Nearly two hours were spent recovering from the trail collapse. Ki and Barefoot assessed the situation and decided on backing down the trail to pitch camp in a protected spot.

"I'm goin' on ahead!" asserted Sam Judd. "I'm gonna find the man that killed my brother. Anybody wanna come along, fine."

"Be a damn sight wiser to stay on," said Barefoot. "I ain't a-fixin' to let them varmints get any farther with the girl, but we'd be a damn sight better off staying together."

"I ain't turning back," the boy said forcefully.

"And I ain't neither," Boyd responded. "But these men are bad hurt and could freeze, we don't get 'em looked after. You wanna go on ahead alone, I reckon I can't stop you, but it seems you're looking for to be a ghost right quick."

The kid worked his jaw as he looked back at the treacherous slope. He nodded once and carefully drew his mount around on the trail.

The men behind him struggled to put the wounded men on horseback. There was no way to protect Ed's bad leg; it was a blessing he remained unconscious. As they all began to move back, McClung and Branch fetched the last of the scattered supplies and cookware. Much had been lost.

Inching along the obscure path with the wind and snow in their eyes, most of the men welcomed the decision to find safer ground. Camp was pitched where a stand of firs gave protection from the wind. They chose a place to erect lean-tos. Ki rummaged through the salvaged supplies, bent on finding the laudanum Dr. MacNaughton had provided.

Night fell bitter, like a cheated prospector; cold, like a twice-jilted woman; dark as the blood that clotted upon Ed's trousers. A fire was kept at the wide side of the shelter, but little wood could be found, and it burned low and cool. Robbie had awakened from his stupor once the fire had put some warmth back into his shocked and bruised frame. Cut up and sore, he miraculously escaped any major injury, though suffering a far worse spill than the sorry cowpunch with his arm in a sling. To a man, they all fell into exhausted, dreamless slumber early in the night. By morning the fire was cold and dead—just like Ed, the fallen rider. His ashen, slack-jawed face greeted the day bejeweled with icy crystals and dim, half-closed eyes. He never benefitted from MacNaughton's forethought.

"I need a volunteer to ride with these men back to Sarah do-rectly."

As a light snow continued to fall in the soft morning light, Barefoot thought more men would have jumped at his request. Young Sam Judd stared at the others with disapproving eyes, wondering who would be coward enough. "McClung," Barefoot called out, surprising the short young man. "In'erested?"

McClung thought and shook his head. "Naw, Marshal. I'm with you."

"Right," said Barefoot, "but I'm only a deputy. Anybody?"

"I think we should all turn back," said a bearded man through chattering teeth. "This weather got us beat this time. I say we try again when things clear up some."

Barefoot replied, "That could be months, Owen. Might could snow up here anytime 'tween 'now and spring. We stand a better chance catchin' 'em holed up now. You wanna escort these men back, here's your chance."

Embarrassed, Owen shook his downturned head and declined.

"You sending Ed back, too, Deputy?" a surprised Sam Judd asked. Barefoot considered it, then suggested burying the man right where they stood, an idea they struck down. Without shovels the frozen ground would defeat them there, too. They decided to send him home across the back of a horse.

A tough-looking cowpunch who knew the country volunteered for the journey. Barefoot was pleased only because he packed a weapon Barefoot felt was unreliable, and of no use to him: an open-frame 1860 Colt Army converted for metal cartridge. Barefoot himself had owned one a few years back and knew it well. His had been a C. B. Richards conversion, and if it didn't jam when lead was flying, it leaked fire at the breech. Barefoot didn't need men dying for that.

With few words the men wrapped Ed's body in his own blanket and secured him to the latigo with rope. The volunteer doubled up with the one-armed rider, whose chance of staying saddled was only a bit worse than Robbie's. It was a sorry funeral procession Ki watched as they receded into the thin gray veil of slow-falling snow.

Barefoot announced, "Mount up, fellas. It's a late start this morn. Let's cut some mud."

Scouting ahead, they found an alternate path across the talus slope above the collapse, taking it cautiously, leading their mounts on foot. Their eyes wandered timidly toward the snow-covered carcasses resting in the gully bottom. Owen tried desperately to keep his hands in his pockets, since the only gloves he owned had their fingers cut off. Ki looked back with concern when, more than once, he heard the poor man curse.

Taking up the rear, young Judd wore a woolen scarf wrapped over his face, so that only his eyes were exposed. Owen rode ahead of him, knocking back a jolt of swill now and then from a flask. There were only occasional moments of relief from the biting wind, as when their trail stayed low on the slope, or hugged steep outcrops, or passed close to a line of trees. Descending into the top of a draw where the wind abated, Owen turned to offer Judd his flask, but the kid declined. Owen took another swallow and began to recap it. It slipped from his hand and dropped to the snow. Pulling himself out of Judd's way with an oath, he dismounted, throwing an embarrassed glance at the boy.

"Y'all right?" Judd checked.

"Damn hands is froze." He retrieved the flask and mounted. "Thought a few nips might warm the blood some, but it ain't doing a lick." Judd realized that Owen's face was raw and stiff with cold. He unwrapped his scarf and said, "Here! Put this on awhile," and threw it to the suffering man. Owen wasn't good at accepting help, but he barely hesitated putting it on.

"Appreciate that, Sam," he said, and mounted up.

They camped in the lee of the tree line as the snowfall ended, while there was still some light. Barefoot was growing irritable, and he wasn't the only one. Several men, including Owen, were questioning the wisdom of continuing, but Ki and Barefoot were confident of themselves and the need to persevere.

Nonetheless, each man fell to the task of building shelters. First they stamped the snow down firmly between two pairs of trees, then set to cutting green boughs. These were set on the packed snow, as ground insulation. They lashed a trimmed tree limb between each pair of trees, draped canvas over them, and leaned boughs and brush against them to complete the lean-tos. Close by, two other men lashed together a triangular frame, over which they draped canvas. After staking down the corners and sides of the fabric, they kindled a small fire at the open end. Owen, meanwhile, offered to slice a slab of bacon, keeping his flask within reach, but his frozen fingers rebelled, and Sam completed the task. They scrounged for wood, taking some green wood from surrounding trees, and prepared a cook fire on the open side of the two branch lean-tos. As night descended, the eight outriders settled down to dry their wet clothing by the fires.

"This all the coffee we got?" asked Bartlett, a top hand originally from around Kerrville. He held up a tin of Arbuckle's containing less than two pots' worth.

Bartlett was a veteran wrangler, a reliable trail boss who didn't take much guff, whether from a rampaging ladino or a rebellious line rider. Working as a brush-popper practically since he first climbed into a saddle, he was a hard-bitten range boss who knew cow geography better than most. He also knew when things were turning sour. When half the chuck was lost, Bartlett could get fairly sour himself.

Barefoot was surprised. "Don't know," he replied. "Should be plenty, unless it's still back there—"

"Ain't a goddamn bit more than this!" Bartlett yelled, throwing the tin to the ground. "Ain't enough chuck in these packs to feed half of us for two days, and you're too damn green to have the least notion how far them hellions done gone!"

Ki stepped in. "No need to get ill, mister," he said quietly. "You volunteered for this."

"I didn't volunteer to die in these hills, and I sure as hell ain't gonna take that kind of shit from some slick-ear muley like you, neither."

Ki looked at him squarely. Bartlett was half a head taller and twice as wide. Ki didn't want to make him an enemy—at least not before they found Jessie. He said, "We got a job to do. You got a problem with how it's getting done, we'd all be better off if you turned back now."

"You calling me a quitter, cuz?"

"I don't call nobody a quitter 'til that's what he decides to do," Ki replied.

The air was tense, and neither man wanted to be the first to back down. Barefoot didn't like it, and Bartlett's original complaint was legitimate. The deputy acknowledged that the situation wasn't great, but that he himself, Ki, and anyone else who wanted to, would continue. He asked Bartlett to stay on; he needed all the help he could get.

Owen cut in, "Wood ain't burning any slower, boys. We best git cookin'."

Bartlett's eyes moved uneasily between Ki and the deputy until, finally, he said, "If we don't find 'em in a day, I say we turn back. I ain't no quitter. Just makes good sense."

Ki took a turn managing the fires during the night. Thankful for the stillness of the air, he became depressed as the prospect of success became more and more remote. Toward first light, snow began to fall once more and, with it, hope.

While breaking camp in the morning, Owen called to Sam Judd. "You seen my knife, Sam? Don't know where I set it." The bearded man looked pale, and he was shivering. Sam stayed close by him as they rode on, kept him talking. When Owen offered to return his scarf, Sam said, "I'm fine, Owen. You wear it."

Though the intermittent snow ceased soon after they started, a frigid wind picked up and screamed across the ridge tops. With faces wrapped, the posse made a dark procession through a land of stark whiteness. Around midday they passed through the crease above the gorge. Shadow was already beginning to envelope the valley bottom. As they crested the rise, the swashing of the stream below burst upon their ears and before them stood the cut, and the footbridge below the craggy sluice. The wind-driven snow had eradicated any sign of animal tracks, but the trail through the cut didn't take a tracker to follow. Once on the rocky opposite bank, the posse broke for a rest amid the trees. Owen stumbled from his horse and tried to hitch it to a sapling. His hands jerked out of control. "M-my f-flask," he asked, "you got it, S-Sam?"

Judd could tell Owen was losing it. He was moving slowly, as if dazed, and while the others tended to the meal Owen's shivering decreased noticeably. An odd stillness was overtaking him. The cold had got to his brain. That's when Owen began asking Sam how his brother Howie was doing these days.

"Howie's dead, Owen. What are you talking about? You all right?" Owen's slurred assurances that he was fine frightened the kid. Sam feared that he was watching a man die before his very eyes.

"Boyd!" he cried. "Come quick!"

Barefoot called off the search. He put one hand inside Owen's clothing, against his skin, and ordered, "Keep him outta the wind. Sam, start a fire over here, quick!"

Barefoot spread his bedroll on the ground behind some thick brush and covered it with woolen blankets and a canvas tarpaulin on top. He ordered Sam to melt snow in the coffeepot and keep it warm. Then he began to strip off Owen's clothes. When the man was naked, Barefoot helped him into the bedroll. "Bartlett!" he called out, "take your clothes off and get inside my soogans."

"Scratch my hairy ass, you sick bastard!" he snapped back. "This man's nearly froze to death and you want me to bed down with you *naked*? Fat chance!"

"Ki!" Barefoot cried, "he ain't gonna last another night like this." Ki began undoing his clothing.

In disgust Bartlett trudged away as Barefoot stripped also. He and Ki joined Owen beneath the covers, and they drew them well over their heads to keep their warm breath inside. In all his years on the range the gruff trail veteran Bartlett had never spent enough time away from sunburnt lowlands to understand what Barefoot and Ki were up to—or he was just too proud to get involved.

At first, Owen seemed to pass deeper into his stupor. As soon as Judd had the fire started, Barefoot directed him to feed Owen cups of warm water, as much as he could take, and before very long the exposed man began showing signs of returned awareness and vigor. Bartlett was man enough to realize, too late, what was happening and avoided making any remarks about the three naked men—unlike some of the others.

"Don't see much happening in there, fellas," mocked one of them. "Thought I'd at least hear some heavy breathing by now."

After nearly an hour had passed, Bartlett complained they had wasted the day. Barefoot ignored him, suggesting they camp for the night, since the lay of the land was good. Soon he and the other two climbed out of the bedroll, to the mostly good-natured razzing of the crew. They dressed themselves, taking care to put dry woolens on Owen, and sat him before the fire with a tarp tented over his head to catch the heat. He ate warm food while the others secured shelter. Turning to Sam, he laid a surprisingly warm hand on his wrist and thanked him.

Morning. The most recent snowfall had filled in their quarry's hoofprints, but the depression left by so many horses was still readily apparent. Pointing out the obvious, Barefoot told his pards that, if the weather should hold out, they'd be on top of their men within hours. He was sure of it. The search was on once more.

Minutes after they got under way, it snowed again—more heavily than ever.

★

Chapter 9

A brown trickle of tonsil varnish dribbled down C. J. Swann's stubbled chin at the sight of Jessie's bonds. He and Dupree came to their feet simultaneously, and when Swann stood next to Tatum, he said, "Take a drink, hoss."

"Sure!" Tatum said, and took the bottle. Swann, in turn, took the bonds and the saddlebag.

"Now, what have we here?" he jeered, bloodshot eyes turned toward Jessie. He riffled through the sheaf in hand and smiled at the huge number of certificates. Reaching into the saddlebag, he gave a hoot of surprise and pulled out another one, equally large. His laughter came from deep within his worthless soul. "Bonds?" he twittered.

"They're worthless to you," Jessie lied. "They're nonnegotiable and registered to me."

Swann read from the face of one certificate: " '*Pay to the Bearer*'?" He guffawed so forcefully his face reddened. He spun around on his heels, swinging fanned-out handfuls of the papers like wings and kicking everything in sight. "Great star of Texas!" he shouted at the top of his lungs, "We have just struck *gold*! Wilfredo Vargas, you can stick your old man's rotting corpse right up your ass!"

"How much is it?" Dupree asked anxiously. "How much?"

Swann riffled through them again and shook his head in disbelief. "I'll be damned if there ain't at least nine or ten . . . It's a goddamn fortune!"

Suddenly a change came over his face. He jammed the bonds back into the bag. His eyes narrowed somewhat, and he levelled them at Jessie.

In a low, threatening voice: "You do realize, little lady, that this changes everything!"

A chill ran down her spine, and she swallowed hard, unable to react. Sure, the money came to an untold fortune for men like these. To Swann, that could only mean one thing: her life was now worthless.

Tatum exhaled after swallowing a long draft of Swann's whiskey and held it out for him to take. "Here you go, Ceej. Man, that stuff sure burns!" Swann swiped the bottle from his hand and headed back to his cot. Tatum said, "Lemme see the bag, Ceej. I want to know how much I found."

Swann simply plopped down on his cot holding the bag, wearing a wide smile. He muttered, "Yeah, sure," and took a drink.

Dupree's insides tickled. He had never held more than eighty dollars in his hands at any one time, and, while he had a fair head for numbers, magnitudes in the thousands left him dazed and confused.

"How much is that apiece?" he asked.

Tatum scowled. "What do mean, 'apiece'? I found that there bag. It's mine, fair and square!"

"You can't be serious," Dupree whined. "There's more there than you could use in you entire life. Besides, we deserve a share."

"For what?" Tatum yelled. "Bein' too dumb to see she was hidin' something? I was the one what knew she was up to something sly. She coulda walked on outta here naked, and you fellers wouldn'ta seen a thing!"

Dupree turned and said, "C.J., tell this guy what the deal is."

"I'll tell ya," he said with a sneer. "I told you once before: things have changed."

"Yeah, so what's our share?" Tatum demanded.

Swann hesitated. He had lied to both of them. Rojas had offered to pay each of Swann's men two hundred in gold, but Dupree expected three hundred; Tatum, only one.

"Three hundred in gold apiece," Swann said slowly. "Minus the one or two hundred I lied about."

Astonishment blanked their faces.

"What in hell you spouting now?" Dupree whispered.

"You sorry pantywaists agreed to do a job: you for three hundred and Tatum for one. Thing is, Vargas offered two each, but I ain't paying more then three all told. I gotta git paid, too, you know." To Dupree he said, "I lied 'cause I knew you wouldn't do it for less," and to Tatum, "and I knew you wouldn't know the difference. But this here's my job. You two work for me. You agreed to a price. What comes out of it extra is mine to do with as I damn well please."

"You lying son of a bitch!" Dupree cried, taking a step toward him.

Swann reached for the Smith & Wesson Russian he kept under his pillow, but before he got his hands near it, the octagonal barrel of Dupree's Remington belt revolver was pointed right at Swann's stony heart.

"Ain't gonna be no shooting," Dupree warned, "and if you think you're gonna make off with all those bonds without cutting us in, you got another think coming."

Swann's eyes glimmered madly, and he hissed through broken and blackened teeth, "Go ahead, bed wetter, shoot. Pull the trigger! 'Cause that's the only way this is ever really gonna git settled."

"Get up, away from your gun," Dupree ordered.

Swann just smirked and said, "Make me."

Dupree's bluff was being called, and even he wasn't sure if he could back his play.

"Tatum," he called, "take his gun."

The Adam's apple on Tatum's craned neck leaped at the thought, but with one more goad from Dupree, the scrawny insect of a man came forward. Swann reached beneath his pillow, but Tatum grabbed his arm before he made it. Fast as a rattler, Swann gave him a hard knee to the ribs, dropping Tatum upon the cot beside him. Swann yanked him to the floor by his shirt, then reached for his pistol. It was gone.

"Lookin' for this, Ceej?" Tatum lay propped on one elbow, pointing Swann's own gun at his disgusting, scarred head.

Dupree talked calmly, telling Tatum to ease off, not to fire. They didn't want anyone killed. They all just wanted what was coming to them. He said they had to stick together, not lose their heads. Not get too greedy.

"I ain't greedy!" Tatum said. "It's mine 'cause I found it!"

Dupree replied, "I don't wanna argue with you, Tatum, but face it: you wouldn't have found anything if it weren't for all of us working together, one way or another. It just wouldn't have happened."

Tatum stammered and shook his head like a stubborn child. Dupree assured Tatum that nothing had to be decided yet; but the first thing to do was to control all the firearms, to keep them out of Swann's reach.

"So you can kill me, right?" Swann grumbled. "So you cin vamoose with all the money to yourselves, right? Then you could put a gun in my hand for the marshal to find and you can have a clear conscience." He laughed demonically. "Kill me now, coward."

"Ain't nobody gettin' killed! Ain't nothing need deciding now," Dupree repeated, and nothing was decided. The three desperadoes soon settled down into an uneasy quiet. The saddlebag full of bonds was placed on the table in the middle of the room, enticingly, teasingly present. It was getting late very slowly, and soon time was measured by the squeak of the cots.

Jessie's heart beat less excitedly now that a stalemate had been achieved. There didn't seem the chance that any one man would be able to make a successful play, since one man was unarmed, one unwilling to murder, and one incapable of effective action. She lay on her stomach at the edge of her lumpy mattress, blackening the floorboard beneath with a charred stick of wood. The men's nerves, she felt, must have been fiddle-string taut.

"You men must realize," Jessie said, "there's probably a posse out looking for y'all by now."

Tatum hissed. "Why don't you hush, lady!"

"The marshal knew where we were headed when you ambushed us," she persisted, "and he was instructed to check on our arrival." All was silent but the howling wind across the eaves. "You killed two men, maybe three."

"I said, why don't you just shut up, lady," Tatum whined.

"And you fired first at one of them," she said to Tatum.

Tatum yelled, "Shut it! C.J., tell her to shut it."

"I doubt the law's going to look kindly on any of you," she finished.

Swann choked out words that could barely be understood. "Little lady seems to think that bevy of saddle tramps back in Sarah can find their way up here in the snow. They can't hardly find their own assholes without a mirror." He put his bottle to his grizzly face and chugged. It plopped when he set it down, and he wiped his mouth with his sleeve.

After a while he said, "All right, boys, you win. We'll split it. Ain't nothing I can do against two of you dung heaps."

"It's only fair," Dupree said. "We ain't asking for nothing we don't deserve."

Tatum's mind was moving in other directions. "Maybe we should make a move, in case there is a posse."

While Swann absently scratched his crotch Dupree said, "What kind of move?"

"That old hut just over the next rise. The one you told me about, C.J."

Swann didn't appear to want to hear it. The hut Tatum referred to was a jacal, a low-down, dirt-floored stone hovel, not much better than a stable, built ages ago by a lone miner who had poked around these hills for years. Like the cabin, it stood on Vargas-controlled land. The hermit miner was long gone, but Swann used it in warmer seasons, on those occasions when the climate—usually in the form of town marshals—got a bit too close for him. He didn't think the cabin would be any worse than the jacal.

Then the words Jessie feared all along came from Dupree's mouth.

"But what about the girl?"

She didn't need to hear it said to know the Ayes and Nays of the situation. Where she erred was to expect Dupree to buy her some time. Swann didn't surprise anyone by saying they had no use for her— "Kill her," he said. Dupree at least was positive he didn't want to do that, and his reluctance to kill anyone outright came across to Tatum as contagious fear. Tatum's wide insect eyes flitted between the two other men, his insect claws brushed his nose and mouth, a bug preening itself. Dupree wanted nothing more to do with Jessie. He wanted to be clean of the entire mess and take his chances heading north and west for as long as he could travel—provided he got his share of the bonds. Swann thought that was fine: leave the girl with "that shit-for-brains" Tatum, give him his share, and say good-bye, but Tatum would have none of it. He wouldn't know what to do with her except abandon her. Swann said he'd probably die of exposure, since he was (as Swann put it) completely ignorant of how to wipe his own ass, never mind how to survive the mountains in winter. In the end, all the conversation proved was that C.J. Swann had an undying obsession with excrement.

He concluded with a lengthy yawn, "She'll be our insurance for a while, might keep us alive. Once we're on our way, then . . ." With a sly raised eyebrow and a tip of his head he let his voice trail off into the obvious. Convincing these scallywags to move to the jacal seemed to Jessie to be the best delaying tactic possible.

"You know, Mr. Swann, why I'm so certain we'll be hearing from a posse very soon?" At the sound of his grunt she said, "Because the first man you killed was my bodyguard. And he was with me because those bonds belong collectively to the largest cattlemen's association in this half of the state. In other words, you're about to have every major landowner and their top guns looking to drill holes through your hides, each one of you." Her lie had little effect.

"Well, they kin join all the other hard cases who are after my butt," Swann scoffed, but Jessie thought she saw in his eyes a subtle weakening, a well-concealed collapse of his defenses, a flash of insecurity. "They'll have a good time finding us. I know these hills better than I know myself, and ain't nobody comin' anytime soon."

They grew tired of talking in circles. It was late, and come daylight, they had much to think about, and possibly even more to do, now that circumstances had so drastically altered. Swann asked two favors of his two accomplices, and Dupree could tell he was desperate by how he asked them: he called each of them by their names. Tatum he asked to douse the lamp so they could all get some shut-eye. Of Dupree, "a man of honor," he asked, and got, a promise: that they would not kill him in his sleep.

When Dupree came inside from his last piss of the day, he announced that snow had begun to fall once again.

Dim shafts of orange light danced through the vents of the wood stove, snoring of men the primitive accompaniment. A stillness, the silencing smell of wood smoke, slumbered over the room, closing the eyes and minds of the refugees who shared it. Warm beneath their buffalo hides and wool, bound by clothing they had worn for days, the sleepers dreamed while wind caressed their shelter and shuddered the door, while icy crystals tapped across the window, while secretive snow blanketed the world and concealed their hideaway in ever deadening quiet.

The creak of wood. The tinkle of glass. The raging phlegm-choked bark of a mad-dog killer in an uncontrollable rage erupted like an earth tremor, brutally yanking Jessie out of her slumber with a heart so pounding and convulsed she thought her chest would burst. Table and chairs stuttered across the floorboards and bashed against her cot as the shadowy bulk of two men locked in blood-simple rage toppled through the room, shattering the silence within their snowbound cocoon.

Curses flew with a force to sear the throat, then the booming skyborne voice of Dupree trying to part the sea of violence. Jessie realized it was Swann and Tatum going at it. Fists swung with the sound of hawks' wings through the darkness, punctuated by shuddering retches and the crack of bone. Glass shattered with a liquid *plosh*; something heavy hit the floor. As Jessie and Dupree tried to protect themselves from the human avalanche Tatum's screeching voice burned their ears while Swann heaped condemnations upon him for daring to double-cross him.

Tatum pulled himself away, pulled a chair in front of himself, and backed against the rear wall, his head crammed underneath the shelf, his feet skidding across the floorboards, his hands shaking uncontrollably. Jessie threw open the stove and lit a piece of torchwood, found the oil lamp, and lit it. Tatum was fully clothed for the outdoors. Coat, hat, gloves—and saddlebag stuck under his arm. His Springfield lay on the floor, where it fell. Swann stood before him, panting and salivating like a hunger-maddened lion before the chair of his tamer.

"You filthy son of a bitch! You ain't gonna need money ever again," in a breathy, rumbling voice.

108

He demanded the bonds once. Not getting them, he demanded them again as he circled toward the wood stove. Demanded a third time as he picked up a split log. A thunderous roar rose as he lunged, drawing the log over his shoulder. Tatum screamed when the first blow broke a leg off the chair, again when the second blow splintered the others, again when the chair came free of his hands, again just before the high-arcing bludgeon came crashing down on his shoulder, severing his collarbone, popping his shoulder joint, slamming him face first to the floor.

"Steal from me!" Swann roared, lifting one foot and mashing it down on the back of Tatum's neck. Jessie heard gurgling in Tatum's throat. Dupree yelled for him to stop, but Swann raised his leg again. "I'll kill you!" and drummed his head again.

"Swann!" yelled Dupree.

The enraged murderer turned, cursing the stupidity of a man who would try to steal the bonds and who dared to steal his whiskey, too, despite his warnings. He climbed over Dupree's cot and rummaged for a weapon. Lifting Brant Adams' Henry, he faced Tatum again and ordered him to his feet. He screeched hoarsely when Tatum couldn't get up on his elbows.

"Enough, Swann!" cried Dupree, careful to keep clear of the Yellow Boy's muzzle. "You've hurt him enough. Leave him be!"

"Git up!" growled Swann. "On your feet, worm."

The battered man lifted himself on his good arm but nearly fainted from the pain. His bloodied face glistened with tears and snot, his mouth enclosed a tangle of shattered white stubs and torn gums. "I can't," he gasped. His drooping chin was raised by the barrel of the rifle. "Can't."

"You was gonna make off with the bonds, right?"

Tatum shook his head feebly.

"You tried to steal my whiskey, right?"

His head knocked back against the wall.

"You was gonna steal our horses, too. Strand us here in this shit hole, am I right?"

Tatum mouthed his denial; no words came out.

"You're a lowdown piece of dried-out shit."

The slits of Tatum's eyes widened slightly. He sighed. "My money . . . Fuck you."

Swann squeezed; the gun erupted. A bullet rammed through Tatum's forehead and into the wall behind. A sickening red splash. His head fell heavily, his body following in a forward slump. Jessie averted her eyes, never seeing the brief shudder of Tatum's extremities.

Dupree was livid with anger but too scared to do anything about it. Swann's face was lit with madness; he salivated with lust. Dupree backed away a step, fearing for his own life, when, surprisingly, Swann said, "We gotta git outta here. Posse'll be here soon. Mighta heard the shot."

Has he snapped? Jessie wondered. She huddled against the wall almost behind the stove, atop a piece of wood. Her mind reeled back to the shot that sent Ki's horse falling on its side, blood spraying skyward as it fell, Swann turning menacingly while the cylinder of his gun moved in time to his finger and the hammer, the horses all about her rearing and flinching, their manes wild, like dark, wind-blown fire, the two men appearing out of the barren fastness behind them. Then she sprung forward again and scrambled for the blankets and hid on her cot as Swann prompted them to clear out of the cabin immediately, despite the howling wind outside, despite the darkness, despite the continually falling snow. She eyed the peachwood grips of her Colt, protruding from Dupree's coat pocket, and his war bag beneath his coat. Ordered to help pack the horses with as much foodstuffs and blankets as she could carry, she endured the shoving and jeering of the maddened killer as he barked orders and scattered unneeded items about the floor. He picked up Tatum's Springfield and his army-issue bandolier, shouting, "Firewood! Don't forget to pack some firewood!" She hoped for a single moment alone in the cabin to retrieve her Colt, but the two men were never outside together at one time. She didn't have time to make a run for

110

it while rigging the horses. They were in and out of the cabin repeatedly, busily rolling blankets, stuffing clothing, stowing ammo, buckling straps, tying laces. When they were about to mount, Swann remembered the horse feed. To Dupree's amazement, he ran back inside, himself, to bring it out.

It was impossible to see anything more than ten feet ahead, but Swann had the way memorized. Rounding the slope behind the cabin and turning into the draw, they moved upward, sometimes wandering into snow-drifts that buried the animals to the knees, then veering out again into lower depths of wind-battered coverage.

Jessie estimated it couldn't have been more than a quarter-mile to the jacal, a long, low stone structure with a swaybacked peaked roof of wattle, daub, and thatching, supported by old cut logs and branches. A wood-plank door to the left of the center pole closed an entrance shaped to the pitch of the roof. Swann leaped from his saddle and tried the latch. He rapped the frozen latch with the butt of his pistol, scraped snow away with the side of his foot, and pulled. Ice and snow feathered down across the gaping darkness. They all dismounted and moved in.

Near the front the roof beams were too low to stand under, but they swayed upward slightly toward the rear as the dirt floor sunk down. At the back stood a small, rusted wood stove, its flue angling out the rear wall. Dupree struck a match and lit the lantern. Shadows were deep across the loosely fitted stone wall.

"It's a stable," he grumbled.

"It'll keep us alive," said Swann, "at least for a while."

★

Chapter 10

Like a bloodhound, Barefoot led the posse straight to Swann's campsite. The burned and broken tree limbs, the scarred earth beneath the snow, the recent fire circle were as plain as day. They were signs of hope to Ki, spurs to action for Sam Judd, and nothing but a thorny challenge to Bartlett and the others—especially Owen, wrapped nervously in thick wools and leathers—who viewed the search as an exercise in futility.

Silently, blindingly, searingly, the crystal knives of white continued to materialize from the steel-gray sky, depositing an ever thickening blanket of protection for the fugitive kidnappers to hide behind. But steadily the posse advanced like bloodhounds.

Sam Judd remarked that with a name like Barefoot and such a knack for tracking, he must have some native blood in him, but the reserved leader denied having any. Ki suspected otherwise, remembering what it was like when he, himself, was new to America: the feelings of isolation, of being an outcast; the jealousy, bitterness, even anger—

especially when someone who was probably in the country for less than a generation himself abused Ki for being a foreigner, something less human than Irish, or Swedish, or German, or English, or what have you. How much worse could it be, Ki wondered, for a man to be outcast in his native land. *I probably wouldn't admit being Indian either,* Ki thought.

It took Sam Judd, riding several places back from the lead, a few moments to realize that Barefoot and Ki had halted. The riders gathered together at the crest of the slope. Following Barefoot's eyes, Judd and Ki looked outward through the snowy veil. Small trees loomed like dark mountain ghosts in the mist. Ki squinted in the wind. Obscure straight lines of a roof, a chimney pipe, a door . . . looming just over the next mound of whiteness. A weak wisp of white smoke briefly hung over the cabin roof before being ripped away by the wind.

Ki deployed his men in three directions, keeping the sharpest long shooters back and with a clear sight of the front door. Barefoot led young Judd and one other in a wide circle to the left, Ki and two others to the right. They slowly tightened the loop like a noose, guns drawn. Barefoot noticed how Judd's hands shook. It was cold as hell fire. Barefoot and Ki, approaching from opposite sides, dismounted, and advanced upon the cabin while two other riders checked the rear. It was too dark inside to see through the filthy frosted windows.

Barefoot crouched beside the door and rapped on it with the grip of his pistol. After listening, he gently undid the iron latch. With a swift motion he shoved the door open, fell back behind the wall, and waited . . . for nothing but silence. He waved the men closer to the empty cabin, and they entered to find the shambles Swann had left, including Tatum's frigid corpse.

Each man swore as he caught sight of it. The place reeked of bad whiskey, wood smoke, and old sweat. On one knee, Barefoot looked Tatum in the face and dipped a finger in the blood behind him. Taking a look at Tatum's pallid face, Ki recognized him, but had trouble placing him. Finally it came to him: this was the imbecile at Stewart's livery who didn't know a mare from a mackerel. Pieces seemed to fall into unsettling places.

The smoldering fire in the stove was just enough to have kept the body from freezing, but not the blood, which had frosted over before it dried. Casting a careful eye about him, Barefoot lifted the coffeepot from the stove and swirled it. The coffee sloshed inside. A greasy skillet on the stove still had crumbs in it. Tin plates and utensils littered the floor beyond the toppled table. Tatum's belongings lay scattered. Judging by the amount of embers in the stove, there had been people in the room right up until the night before. He figured Tatum hadn't been dead for more than ten or twelve hours.

"These boys done left in a swivet," he concluded.

"Could Miss Jessie do something like this?" asked Judd, looking over the wreckage.

Ki replied, "She's capable of it, especially when the furniture's this ugly. But I doubt it this time. Not her style. That man's unarmed, and he don't look to be a match for her." Barefoot looked surprised. "That's right," Ki explained. "She can be mighty feisty when she's got a mind to be." He added, "Boys, you might keep an eye out for a pair of fine leather saddlebags. They belong to Miss Starbuck."

Barefoot knelt to look beneath the cot nearest the door. A deck of cards, some dented tins, some soiled clothing. A few small pieces of paper scattered around the table caught his eye. In Dupree's neat handwriting three names he was thrilled to see together: Dupree, Tatum, and Vargas. He gathered as many of the papers as he could see and stuffed them into his shirt pocket. Then he swept his eyes across the floor to the opposite wall and noticed something gleam beneath some discarded cloth. Long and straight, the glint of brass. He recognized the receiver of the Yellow Boy right off and fetched it with a sense of triumph.

"Damn stupid to leave this behind," he said, opening the receiver and the fully loaded magazine.

"Hey, Boyd," Ki called, over by the stove, "look at this!"

On a flat wallstone almost behind the stovepipe was a message scrawled in charcoal, as if with the end of a charred stick:

BB
OK
J—

"Now, that is Jessie's style," Ki said. "I'd bet an eagle that's hers."

"Let's get on it," Boyd announced.

"We ain't gittin' on nothin'."

Ki and Boyd turned and saw Bartlett, Owen, and three others standing tall by the door.

"How's that?" Ki replied.

Bartlett, in a serious voice: "I said, we ain't gittin' on nothin'. We ain't goin' no further. Them coyotes done gone, put that poor bastard down, and evidently vamoosed clear outta this place. And that's what we intend doing, too."

"All of you?" said Boyd.

McClung and his large sidekick, Branch, looked around and stepped away from Bartlett. Branch said, "We're still riding, Deputy. We're game."

"Me, too," said Sam Judd.

Softly Barefoot said, "Owen? You turnin' back?"

The fearful man swallowed and tried to speak, but only nodded instead. In the silence he was heard to whisper, "Sorry."

Ki stared at them. Three men turning back. That left five to continue the hunt, and that was good enough for him. He would ride on even if he had to go alone. He wasn't as angry toward Bartlett as he was sorry for Owen; but he certainly felt vindicated: he knew it was only a matter of time before Bartlett turned tail. His eyes must have said so, because Bartlett didn't like the look of them.

Boyd said, "I'd be obliged if you just took with you the supplies you'll need to get back and leave us the rest."

Bartlett sneered. "I ain't unpacking a string just to pack it all up again. We got what we need and you got yours."

"You sure of that?" Ki challenged.

Bartlett's brow dropped, as if he were focusing on a kill.

"I don't know who you think you are," he said, "coming around and making like you're the goddamn sheriff, but I ain't cared for your slant-eyed face the first time I saw it."

Ki wasn't interested in fighting the huge man, didn't feel the need to humiliate him before his peers. He just raised his coat collar and said, "Let's ride, Boyd." He stepped toward the door, but Bartlett stood in his way. "I'm going through this door, Bartlett," he said. "We got a job to do."

"Go ahead," Bartlett snarled, "say it. Say what you're thinking." Ki merely stared him down. "Go on, you little prick, call me a quitter."

Ki uttered, "You said it. Not me."

The big man slapped both of his hands against Ki's chest and heaved. Falling backward, Ki held tightly to Bartlett's wrists, drawing him forward by his own momentum, crouching as he neared the floor and crossing Bartlett's thigh with his ankle. Before the hit the boards, Ki had Bartlett in a somersaulting fall that threw him over his head and sent the big man crashing into the hard edge of the overturned table beyond.

Men scattered. As Ki came to his feet Bartlett instinctively grabbed a chair by the end of one leg and stood wielding it as easily as a small club. The chair came down. Ki lunged and ducked, tackling Bartlett low. The chair crashed harmlessly to the floor, but the two men tumbled to the back of the room. Bartlett's head slammed another chair hard, and a rivulet of blood trickled out of his scalp as he rolled upon Ki, flailing heavy fists and jerking his knees dangerously into Ki's pelvis.

A dizzying blow to the side of Ki's face sent him reeling. Another to his ribs doubled him over where he lay. His forearm slid through Tatum's coagulated blood. Bartlett clutched the first thing his hand could find—the log that had pulverized Tatum's bones. Ki sat up as Bartlett heaved a sidearm blow. In one move, Ki ducked his head and landed a devastating upward thrust with the heel of his hand into Bartlett's crotch, crushing his nuts with numbing accuracy. The log left Bartlett's hand and bashed Tatum's lifeless skull once again, toppling the hunched corpse on its side. Bartlett hit the floor right next to it, clutching his abdomen in speechless agony, turning pale, eyes rolling backward, falling into a dead faint.

Ki staggered to his feet. His face was already showing the bruise, and one sleeve was smeared with the dead man's blood. He anticipated trouble from the other deserters, but none of them wanted to challenge his lightning-fast martial artistry.

Checking his face for blood, he said to Owen, "Get him on a horse when he's fit to ride and send him home where he belongs. Anyone else who's still with me, saddle up. We're losing time."

They bustled out the door into the falling snow. Owen feared for their safety and called out after them. "Boyd! Sam! You can't go on in this snow! Come on back to town—we can try again when the snow clears up some!"

Barefoot shook his head and saddled up as Owen followed them outside.

"But Boyd! What do we do with that dead guy in there?"

"Can't rightly bury him 'til the ground thaws, Owen, so the hell with it; he won't be stinking for some time to come in this cold. Leave him be."

McClung and Branch followed silently as Barefoot led them into the deepening whiteness. Owen yelled

117

after them, getting no response. Soon his voice was obliterated by the moan of the sorrowful, foreboding wind.

Sam Judd spurred his mount alongside Ki's. "Hey, mister!" he said. "You threw that guy like he was a heap of dirty laundry." His voice was tinged with awe, and he stared at the impressive silent warrior more than he looked at where he rode. "Where'd you learn to do that kind of stuff? You some kind of assassin?"

Ki turned to him, surprised by Judd's remark. Being an assassin was the furthest thing from Ki's experience. The years he had spent studying the mysterious arts of the warrior were also spent learning to live according to *bushido,* the warrior's code of honor. *Budo,* the way of the warrior, was more than just fighting, but it was that, too. How could a boy who grew up in the fastness of Texas cattle country understand what it all meant to Ki, who only fought to defend—whether himself or Jessie—no matter how often or how strongly he desired to strike out at a world that continually fenced him out.

"I'm not a killer," was Ki's answer to the impressed young man.

"Aw, come on, you never killed a man?"

Ki's eyes narrowed. He looked away. "I have killed before. But I'm not a killer. Not that kind."

"Do you fight like that all the time?" Judd asked.

"You mean, do I get my face bashed in like I just did?"

Judd laughed. He said he admired how Ki used his hands and feet. Ki replied, "Where I come from, you've got to know those things. When you find yourself without a weapon, your hands and feet may be all you've got."

Without a weapon. With only her wits and her hands. Jessie had to rely on herself as she lay bundled in her bedroll on the floor of the hovel, waiting. Mayhem loomed with the certainty of sunrise. Exhausted by the physical and emotional stress, unable to doze soundly, she nodded on the precipice of sleep, never able to fall, throughout the long night since their move to the jacal.

When the stove was lit, the bedding rolled out, there wasn't much to do but wait in the face of the fact that Swann was prepared to kill for the bonds while Dupree was prepared to defend. It was a cold, frozen standoff ever since the balance was shifted by Tatum's murder. The imminent catastrophe loomed over them like the stalking of a spectral panther as they went clomping through the snow. It engulfed them like the shadow of giant black wings cowling their greed and depravity. Dupree had to remain on guard every second, never allowing himself to doze, not even to nod, knowing Swann would seize the first opportunity to pounce. Every time Dupree's eyes closed or his head drooped, the groaning wind was coupled with Swann's devilish snickering. Swann's craven, grizzled face became even more contorted by the sick thrill he got from anticipating his victory over Dupree, whose only desire was for escape—escape from Swann, escape from these frozen Sierra Diablos, escape from Texas. And with his share of that saddlebag fortune, escape from his entire desperate dirt-poor past. He was sick of his hardscrabble existence, tired of chasing after other men's promises and his own illusions. He was going to snare his share of those bonds if it was the last thing he did on earth.

"C.J." he mumbled. "Listen to me." He stood up and stretched. "Listen. We got to figure this out. Five thousand bucks worth each, C.J. Think about it. That's more than either of us will ever seen again in our lives. Ain't that enough for each of us?"

Swann yawned, but didn't look tired. He stretched, then yawned again. Dupree rubbed his eyes, shook his head, waiting for an anwer.

"I told you," Swann replied, "you work for me. You'll make your money."

"You lied about the money," Dupree insisted. "I've earned a share of those bonds. None of us knew about

119

them when we started into this." Getting no response, he cajoled, "Okay. How about four thousand for me—sixty-forty split. Huh?"

Swann sat up against the wall. Riprap in his throat. "Fifty-fifty, sixty-forty, eighty-twenty—it don't matter what the hell you say. I'll split it with you, and you'll shoot me in the back first chance you git. Maybe you won't even wait that long. You'll wait for me to fall asleep, then drive some lead into me. Right? Yeah, I know how you're thinking. I kin see it in your eyes. You see dollar signs, and all you can think about is figgerin' how to make off with what's mine. Well, I'm going through with this. And I'm gonna git that money Vargas owes me now, then kick him in his lazy ass and never set foot on his turf again."

"You don't know shit, C.J."

"I know I got more balls than you and Tatum put together, and I kin do this right."

Hours crawled by. Dupree kept his head up, his eyes mostly open. Swann stared at him like a predator focused on its prey.

Dupree sat up and breathed deeply. "C.J., give me three thousand worth, and I'll take the girl off your hands. You'll never see us again."

Swann smiled broadly and shook his head with a chuckle. "Price going down, boy? You'll do anything to git some o' what's mine, won't you? The girl has nothing to do with this."

"Then what in hell are we going to do with her?" Dupree asked.

Swann just shrugged. "Kill her. What the hell? We're already good for the gallows if we get caught. . . . Only it sure would be a pity not to partake of her wonderful charms before she became useless." His face brightened with a broken-toothed smile that made Jessie's skin crawl.

"I'll tell you what," he said. "What do you say me and the girl take one little roll in the sheets. I'll pay you what I owe you, then you can have the girl all to yourself. You can do what you want with her. That ain't so bad, is it? I'll bet she'd put a smile on your face no mess o' money in the world could beat."

"Forget it, C.J. I'll take my money, but you ain't laying a hand on her."

Swann stiffened somewhat. He taunted them both. "What are you, some kind of schoolboy? Look at her! Wouldn't you just love to see that fine young thing buck-ass naked? Get your hands on them big, round tits and suck them nipples 'til they're hard?"

"Shut up, C.J."

"C'mon, think on it. That big ol' bush between her legs and that tight, warm thing? Huh, Dupree? Don't tell me you don't want some of that. Ain't you a man? The two of us could take her at once, you—"

"C.J., I swear I won't stand for it," Dupree insisted. "I'd let you take all the bonds before I let you harm the girl. Do it, and, I swear . . ."

"You swear what?" Swann scoffed.

"I swear, C.J., I'll kill you."

Grinding laughter filtered through Swann's crowded throat. He kept his hand always near his Smith & Wesson, knowing that Jessie's slate-gray Colt never left Dupree's palm. Each of them had a second, less reliable gun within reach, and both knew that all it would take to tip the scales a little further was a single well-placed bullet. So they sat, long past the first points of daylight poked through the hut's tiny cracks and crevices.

Jessie's eyes flashed open. Awakened by a noise, she was surprised she had fallen asleep. Swann's bedding was empty. A splashing sound in the darkened front end of the hut. The sight of Swann crouching and pissing in the corner distressed her. Then she blanched.

Dupree was sleeping.

Without turning to face her, Swann whispered, "That boy's dead to the world, you know. Can't hear a thing."

"You killed him?" she gasped.

He laughed. "Not yet." He shook his thing dry and turned, purposely exposing himself to Jessie. He stepped closer. "Listen. If we're real quiet, we could have ourselves a little fun, then I'll be on my way with the bonds. I'll bet he won't even try to stop us. I cin tell ya, he really wants some hisself. What d'ya say, honey?"

He approached with his big thing swaying in front of her, growing out of its darkened foreskin and coming to attention, crooked and nasty as tree bark.

"Whaddya say?"

Fast as a cat, he was upon her, grabbing at her neck while covering her mouth, but she managed a piercing scream. She yelled and tried to kick, but the heavy buffalo hide entrapped her legs. She remembered something Ki had taught her. Folding her fingers in half and keeping her palm open, she jabbed her knuckles into Swann's throat, bashing his trachea and sending him coughing across her legs.

She kicked and pulled and freed her legs, but didn't make it far. Swann rose and punched her in the jaw. Sightless, she fell back with the smell of her own blood in her nose. He lunged, tore open the buckle of her belt, and clawed at the buttons on her denims. The first one popped, then two more, to reveal the delicate flesh of her stomach and bronze wisps of pubic hair. Then, from behind, Dupree pounced.

Sputtering curses, he pistol-whipped the scar-headed man across his shoulder blade. He aimed for his head, but Swann moved like a wounded mountain lion. Swinging his elbow around low, he knocked Dupree off his feet as the pistol *whooshed* past his ear. Like a cudgel, his rock-hard fists drove into Dupree's ribs. Dupree scrambled to strike again with the pistol. Leaping to his feet while holding up his pants, Swann kicked Dupree in the stomach and the ribs, two, three times, rolling the winded man onto his face. Another hard, swift kick to Dupree's unprotected head knocked a tooth from his mouth and left him still, with both hands beneath his battered chest.

Swann turned back to Jessie. She stood in the saddle stance Ki had taught her, hands ready. Swann came at her. She spun, sent her other leg into a circular sweep and kicked Swann's forward foot out from under him, dropping him hard to the ground. The impact stunned him. Regaining her stance, she lifted her foot and drove the heel of her boot down mightily into his face, lacerating lips and tongue against his jagged teeth. She dashed for the door.

Sensing Swann was right behind her, she spun around, wielding a backhand fist. It connected with an audible *chock* that made blood and saliva fly, but still Swann lunged. She caught his wrist and pulled it to herself while stepping out of his way. She pulled him off balance, smashed him in the back of neck with the hardened edge of her hand as he fell, and propelled him helplessly forward, face first, into the cold stone wall.

Blood smeared down the rough stone. On his knees and elbows he grunted like a shot boar while Jessie cast about for a weapon. Swann sprung, rammed her in the stomach, knocked her on her back, across Dupree's outstretched legs. He grabbed her ankles and dragged her, swung her like a sickle, and bashed her against the wall. He kicked her in the ribs and swung her back toward the door. She caught herself on Dupree's bedding. Swann dropped to his knees, straddling her, choking her and winding back his massive fist while she writhed.

"Jessie!" Dupree moaned.

The glint of metal in midair. The weight of iron in her palm. She fumbled. The barrel . . . the hammer . . . grip . . . trigger guard . . . trigger. She fended off his free hand, screamed and squeezed, flinched with the explosion that catapulted the maniac backward, head first, in a spatter of red.

Pulling away, gasping, she looked at Swann lying twisted in the corner. She sat up. Dupree's eyes seemed about to fall out of his head. He looked at Jessie with relief as tears welled in her eyes and she whimpered, not quite crying.

"We gotta get back to the cabin," Dupree said. "If somebody don't find us soon, at least we'll be safer there. Come on!" He tried to take the Colt from her hand, but she pulled it back. He clutched it firmly and took it from her.

It was a struggle to get to her feet. Her ribs ached and her face burned. She pulled her clothing together and circled, as if in a daze.

"You helped me," in a quivering voice. "He would have killed me."

Dupree agreed, but was in a hurry to vacate, to be through with Caddo Jack Swann forever. He went to the body, pushed it over with his boot. Gleaming red shone from the hairy side of Swann's head. Dupree pushed him back down and went to roll up his bedding. He and Jessie caught sight of the saddlebag simultaneously. She stooped for it. He lunged and scooped it off the dirt floor, burning his eyes right through to her soul.

"Quick," he said, "get your bedding on a horse and leave every damn thing else."

"Maybe we should take the other horse," Jessie suggested.

"We don't need it. Move!"

★

Chapter 11

"You hear that?" Sam Judd exclaimed.

"Gunshot." Barefoot said. "Over there!"

Over the delicate whisper of falling snow, the muffled pop was still unmistakable and had to have been close for them to hear it. Their hearts pumped harder, and their hands and feet seemed to warm instantaneously. The rowels of spurs dug into horsehide, and Judd and Barefoot took the lead. With the words, "Come on, fellas!" on his lips, Ki turned to urge on McClung and Branch, only to find them leveling their revolvers at the backs of the advancing riders ahead.

"Get down!" shouted Ki as the first volley erupted. Already in a fast trot, young Judd was struck by McClung's shot high in the back and slumped over the neck of his horse. One foot came out of the stirrup. Another shot rang out, and he slipped off, into the deep snow, lucky enough to catch only one hoof on the fly.

Branch's shot missed its mark, and Ki wasn't about to give him a second try. As Branch fingered back the hammer on his single-action Ki had already snapped off a *shuriken* into the air. Its silvery flash was a shooting star with saw-blade teeth that bit viciously into Branch's neck behind the ear, dumping him to the snow like a tree felled. Enraged and only a little bit dazed, he scurried for cover.

Barefoot, having veered sharply out of the way, rounded a fir and came out the other side, blazing. His first shot drilled clear through the front of McClung's coat, but the second burrowed deep into his flesh. The back-shooter held to the lizzie and fired back twice as he kicked his mare feverishly. His two misses only caused a cloud of snow to burst from the branches of the tree. Two more shots rang out from Barefoot's steady-aimed No. 3. Puffs of snow rose from McClung's coat, telling the tracker that his shots found their marks. As McClung's horse stumbled over a snow-covered obstacle, the back-shooter's limp body bounced raggedly to the ground.

Ki dismounted while on the run and flattened himself in the snow behind a fallen tree trunk. Barefoot meanwhile kept moving until he, too, found cover. They had the bushwhacker Ki had wounded in a crossfire no sane man would challenge.

"Throw out your guns!" ordered Barefoot. "You ain't got a chance!"

The big redhead was bleeding badly from the neck, and it scared him. The reddened snow around him melted and refroze, lurid as a slaughterhouse floor.

"I got more guns than you can handle, Deputy," Branch lied. "I'm riding outta here, or I'm taking both of you to hell with me!"

Ki yelled, "That's just where you're going if you don't do what he says. You ain't in no position to bargain. Throw out your weapons."

Branch panted with fear. His mind squirmed, searching for a plan. McClung lay writhing in the snow several yards off, and he could hear him moaning and coughing.

"Wade?" Branch called. "Wade, you all right?" He saw McClung's dark figure move, as if trying to roll onto his back. "Wade! I need you, man! Let's show these jackasses some shooting! Come on, Wade. You're the best! Just pick up your gun and shoot!"

Coughing muffled by the snow. Thin wisps of vapor from McClung's shallow breathing. No help there, so the redhead decided to bolt.

"Goddamn you all!" he shouted, throwing lead in both directions and running for his life. Barefoot fired once and missed. He spurred his mount and took off after him.

Branch caught sight of his own horse and careened toward it, unaware that Barefoot's mount was already upon him. Startled by Branch's sudden turn, Barefoot's gelding reared up, the deputy held fast; Branch yelled, threw up his gun and fanned off two shots into the dun's chest, tripped on something snow-buried, and fell. The gelding's heart exploded, shot with lead, and the great animal collapsed, rider and all, directly upon the screaming desperado. Lifted off the saddle while in free-fall, Barefoot landed on his side in deep snow, but heard a popping sound unlike any he had ever heard before—the sound of Joe Dell Branch's spine being severed as the dun crushed him upon the snow-hidden tree trunk he had tripped over. The gelding struggled in vain to get up, making Branch's agony infinitely worse, but only for the few moments remaining in his worthless life.

Ki ran to Sam Judd. The two holes in his outer coat seemed too small to take away an entire young life, too insignificant to snuff it out in so brief an instant. But there they were, two holes barely large enough to get a finger into. One great big life seeping away into the air. Ki lifted the kid gently and brushed the snow from his face. He called his name, but saw that the weighty, lifeless corpse was no longer Sam Judd. The boy who had ridden out to avenge his only brother's murder was with his brother now, without ever taking his man, without ever firing a shot, yet dying honorably in the attempt.

Barefoot was rolling McClung over on his back when Ki came alongside. The man was still alive, but barely.

Ki roughly pulled him up by the lapels.

"Who put you up to this?" Ki demanded.

McClung's skin was reddened with cold, and snow matted his face and hair. As his head came up vertical, blood trickled from his slackened mouth. His eyes gradually met Ki's, and he looked about to cry.

"I'm cold," he simpered, "real cold. Help me, please." Ki repeated his question, but McClung answered, "I'm so cold. Please, mister, don't let me die. God, don't let me die here. Not now."

Shaking him angrily, Ki said, "You're dead, damn you! There's not a thing I can do for you. You're gonna to die like the back-shooting varmint you are, right here, right now, where the coyotes will feast on your miserable guts. No one's ever gonna find what's left of you. Now tell me who paid you to kill us—tell me before you go to your maker without a thing to redeem yourself. *Who?*"

A tear slid down the man's cheek. His chin quivered, and he tried to speak. He began to tell his story, then shivered terribly. "God, I'm so cold, please, God, no."

"Who?" with a final shake.

McClung seemed to bit his lip, but with a breath, it turned into a whispered "*Vargas!*"

Ki threw him down before he was dead and walked away.

"Kill me!" pleaded the dying man. "Please kill me. I'm so cold!"

Over his shoulder Ki said, "Fuck you!" and went to find his horse.

"Did you hear that?" Jessie asked excitedly.

"Gunshots." Dupree said. "Over there!"

Despite the susurrus of falling snow, the gunfire was unmistakably close. Dupree hesitated. Like Jessie, he figured a posse had arrived. Why there was shooting, they could only guess—and worry. They mounted their horses, unwilling to be found on foot by either friends or enemies, but Dupree sat motionless, frozen by indecision.

Jessie said to him, "You know as well as I do, good or bad, those shots have something to do with people searching for us. Over all this distance and through all this snow, they've come this far. They ain't going to stop now. If you run, they're going to find you. And if you run off with my bonds, I'll make sure of it."

A driving wave of snow stung their faces, and still Dupree did nothing.

"You saved my life," Jessie continued. "I'll make sure they know that. You may have helped kidnap me, but you haven't harmed anyone. I'll stand up for you. I promise."

Breathing heavily, Dupree nodded and spurred his horse. They made slow progress on the trail toward the cabin and soon rounded the final slope. Ahead of them, two mounted figures and another horse following appeared like ghosts out of the wintry mist. As the figures took on form and clarity Jessie saw that over the third horse was slung a body, feet swaying, hair dangling. That's when she recognized the two pony-tailed men. Her heart leaped.

"Ki! Ki, you're alive!" she screamed with delight.

About to rush ahead to meet them, she paused and turned to Dupree. His face was open, vulnerable. "Here," he said, holding out the saddlebag. Jessie slung it over her lap and said, "Come on."

"Jessie!" Ki yelled back. "You all right?"

Without thinking, Dupree raised his open hands for the men to see. Ki and Jessie leaped from their saddles and embraced.

"You're alive!" she cried. "I thought . . ." Her eyes filled with tears, and she locked her arms around his muscular torso. Ki stood back and looked at her. The darkening bruise on her face concerned him, but she shrugged it off, too happy to see her dearest friend alive.

"What about him?" he asked.

"He's all right," Jessie replied. "He saved me."

"We found one of them dead, back there in the cabin. Where's the priest?"

"Dead, too. There's an old hutch they took me to, back thataway."

Barefoot asked Dupree's name, and the handsome owlhoot told him he was giving himself up, that he hadn't killed anyone. The deputy frisked him down and relieved him of his war bag—cartridges, the old Remington, and Jessie's Colt—then announced that they should head back as soon as possible; the weather wasn't getting any better. He didn't care to risk any more lives by worrying about the dead.

They moved as quickly as the thick snow allowed, hoping to get to lower ground before they all froze to death. Before they reached the killing ground where McClung and Branch lay freezing, Ki explained the circumstances of the kid's death, and who was responsible. Repeatedly the riders shook off their hats and brushed off their shoulders. At one point, Boyd fell back and patted the snow from Judd's frosted body.

They stopped briefly at the cabin to build a fire and warm themselves, dry their boots. Barefoot covered Tatum's body with a blanket. The sun was about as high in the southern sky as it would get. Before long they were again moving on.

Barefoot asked Dupree if he knew a shorter route back to Sarah, and fortunately, he did. It was a minor detour, its best attribute being it allowed them to avoid the deadly slope that held them up three days earlier. They trudged on toward the cut of the gorge.

The snowfall seemed to abate somewhat. Visibility improved, but not the cold. At least their eyes weren't stung by wind-driven needles of ice. They moved slowly down the incline, into the cut. As they emerged from the trees the water looked darker than before, more foreboding. Barefoot led the way across the snow-choked planks, with Jessie following last. They started up the clearing above the embankment just as she crossed the midpoint of the span.

Two shots rang out, echoing like rolling thunder. One struck the bridge just inches in front of Jessie's mount, the other hit Ki's horse in the quarter above one thigh, bringing it down tail-first. Ki cursed in disbelief—it couldn't happen a second time!—and sprung from the stirrups in time to fall clear of the kicking broomtail. Another shot chased Barefoot and Dupree higher across the open slope, while the horse carrying Judd's body tried to break free of the lead hitched to Ki's saddle. A bullet slammed into the planks behind Jessie's horse, preventing her retreat, and it was all she could do to keep the spooked critter standing on the slippery plank bridge.

From somewhere above them, hidden among the crags, a cracked voice boomed and echoed, "Stay where you are, or I'll kill you where you sit! Bitch, drop the bag. Do it!"

Jessie's breath stopped as Dupree screamed out, "Swann? You're dead! She killed you!"

Another blast and the lead passed so close to Dupree's face the whiz made him flinch. He kicked his horse's flanks and put more distance between him and the resurrected madman. Barefoot, keeping an eye on the ridges, saw the gun smoke. He raised his No. 3 and waited. When the voice yelled, "Drop the bag!" he saw a sliver of black move within a V of rock near the peak of the cut. He squeezed twice, but the second hammer strike clicked on an empty chamber.

"Shit!" He had forgotten to reload after the ambush. His one shot drew deadly attention from the gunner above, and he zigzagged up the unprotected slope, buying time to level Brant Adams' Yellow Boy.

"You're dead, bitch!" came the throat-searing cry, and shots rang out in succession. The first one knocked deeply into the wood of the bridge, but the second pierced the the leather saddlebag and embedded itself in the animal's side, just below Jessie's leg. A third hit the horse in the neck, sending it into wild convulsions. Jessie reined in hard, trying to get the animal to turn tail and run into the trees, and when it had nearly made it around, it stumbled and slammed down on one knee. She fumbled for her Colt. Another shot missed. Jessie screamed at the tortured animal, dug

131

her heels deep, driving the broomtail onward toward solid ground.

The Yellow Boy's brass furniture gleamed. The deadly octagonal barrel aimed high. Drawing a deep, steadying breath, Barefoot smelled the machine oil of the well-kept smoke pole. His very first shot put an immediate stop to Swann's barraging of Jessie. He fired twice more, shattering rock from the V in front of Swann's face. Then the Henry would fire no more. Desperately, Barefoot worked the lever. He knew the weapon was loaded. He smacked the receiver and fingered the hammer. The last cartridge had ejected, but none other would feed into position. He turned the weapon over, and there was the problem: the magazine beneath the barrel had been dented near the receiver when it fell from Adams' scabbard, preventing any more ammunition from feeding. Again the fault was his oversight, and again he rode out of firing range. He quickly searched through his saddlebags for more ammunition, only to find two cartridge boxes completely empty. He cursed his own stupidity. He had let McClung and Branch gather the supplies scattered during the trail collapse. Of course there was no ammunition! Still, he had a plan.

By this time, Ki was heating up his own iron, throwing lead steadily and carefully at the V where Swann had revealed himself. But Swann had the advantage. The defenders were on lower, unprotected ground, wide open to Swann's vantage point. Soon Ki was driven back, running on foot toward Dupree and Barefoot. Swann trained his sights once again on Jessie.

Ki steeled himself to watch the focus of his entire life die.

Her horse hobbled to the far end of the bridge, toward the cut. Bullets trailed her all the way. Blood spurted from the animal's croup. Unable to draw a decent bead on her attacker, Jessie curled into as small a target as possible just as another shot rifled through her long hair and into the animal's mane. Mere yards from the woods, the beast toppled, dying.

In a wink Jessie was up, trying to pull the saddlebag from under the beast, but it was stuck fast. Swann's next shot pinned her behind the bulk of the twitching horse, where she pressed herself down lengthwise, Colt in hand.

"You're dead, bonds or no bonds!" echoed the voice. He fired again, aiming for the very edge of the horse's flesh. The Springfield's 70-grain blast propelled a massive 611 grains of lead to carve a bloody gash across the hide of the horse and through the shoulder of Jessie's coat. It was a lucky shot, she knew, because of the Springfield's fierce recoil and frightening muzzle blast. The phony priest was no marksman.

Barefoot was nearly done. He had emptied the Henry of its .44 rimfire pills—the same ammunition he needed for his Smith & Wesson—and was filling the revolver's last chamber when he looked at Ki and said, "All right, let's get her outta there."

Ki snapped the cylinder down on his Peacemaker. Turning to Dupree, he said, "You can do some good that might come back to you, but no guarantees. What do you say, Boyd?"

Barefoot nodded and threw Dupree his Remington. "Spread out."

They fanned out as far as the terrain allowed. As soon as they were in range, Swann fired on them. Staying always on the move, the three defenders managed to force Swann to waste plenty of lead and tire himself in alternating the heavy Springfield with his pistol. What Barefoot and Ki didn't know was how much ammunition Swann actually possessed. Dupree suspected that Swann's bandolier was less than half of it, as there had been boxes more left packed on the horse that he and Jessie unwisely had left at the jacal. Swann fired relentlessly until one after another of the defenders' small weapons began to dry up.

Seeing Barefoot make a galloping foray within pistol range of Swann's position, Jessie decided to bolt. She stood and yanked on the saddlebag one last time. It sprung free. She lost her footing and quickly recovered.

She fled across the bridge toward the men, skidding and sliding in the hindering snow. Firing and reloading the Springfield nearly every five seconds, Swann put up a formidable fusillade, and when Jessie felt another heavy slug pierce the saddlebag flying behind her, she dropped it at the edge of the bridge and ran with every ounce of strength and breath she could muster. Barefoot, circling toward her after his last attack, scooped her beneath his arm when she made it to the slope and carried her uphill in the protection of his horse's lee, with one foot hooked over the cantle. Their ammunition spent, Ki and Dupree fell back, relieved by Jessie's rescue.

The air went silent.

Suddenly, the muffled sound of far-off hooves in the snow rose above the rush of white water. Swann, on horseback, came galloping down through the cut, revolver in hand, heading for the saddlebag.

"No!" Dupree shouted. He spurred his mount madly and plummeted downhill toward the assassin.

"Let him have it!" Jessie cried.

Dupree yelled, "He'll never be seen again!" and raced toward the bridge. The paths of the two obsessed riders converged, but Dupree was faster. Whipping his horse with the reins on either side, he closed in, drawing Swann's extended arm. The gap between the two riders narrowed. Dupree gripped the lizzie and leaned as far down from the saddle as he could, skimming his hand across the frozen surface, hooking up a wake of white spray as his hand clawed at the leather bag . . . and missed. He drew himself up again, pulled hard on the reins to turn back. Two gunshots exploded through the canyon, and Dupree somersaulted backward off the rump of the horse, giving a guffaw that was heard on the slope above.

Circling about, Swann slowed his horse, casually scooped up the saddlebag, and held it up for the helpless onlookers to see. He bellowed a triumphant roar, fired a parting shot that zipped through the trees near where Jessie stood, and galloped across the bridge and into the wooded gully beyond the cut.

"Goddamn hell-bound demon," Barefoot muttered. "Ain't never seen nothing like him in my life."

As Ki ran down to check on Dupree, Jessie squatted, exhausted, and put her face in her hands.

"Thank God he's gone," she sighed.

★

Chapter 12

Widow Pritchard was in her grandmotherly glory. For more than two days she had cared for Jessie and Ki, warming them with hot soup and tea, cooking and baking their meals, washing their clothes. They had slept many long hours upon returning to Sarah, and the town was still drenched in bone-chilling rain that had begun soon after Jessie first disappeared. She was now so gaunt from loss of weight, the widow feared she would fall ill, but young Jessie was as fit as they come. By the third day, she seemed to have bounced right back. And Ki, too.

News of their return spread like wildfire throughout town, and it didn't fail to raise some controversy. What to do, for instance, with three dead bodies that figured in so depraved a series of crimes, frozen on some far-off mountain? Most folks felt the way Ki did: let them set to rot. There were plenty of others, of course, who just couldn't see clear to dishonor even a murderer's body. Even so, no one budged from their cozy cabins and ranch houses to venture into the windy badlands beyond the horizon.

There was one person, in particular, who was surprised by Jessie's return.

After a return journey of just under two days the four riders slogged through the muddy streets on two horses, drenched, withered, on the verge of collapse. Their appearance startled the community—most everyone knew who Jessica Starbuck was—especially because of the grim burden of the trailing third horse. One of the riders, word in the taverns had it, was variously one of the kidnappers, one of the posse volunteers, or a hermit, who had stumbled upon the kidnappers and saved Jessie. His flesh wound was his lucky reward for crossing paths with the back-shooting outlaws. The one or two cowhands who recognized the wounded man as Dupree were in no hurry to admit their acquaintance; instead, they hurried down to Broward's for a few stiff ones to forget ever knowing the loser.

But getting his hair cut the day Jessie returned, in one of those big, cushiony new barber chairs down at Bennett's Tonsorial, was the short, mustachioed man named Rojas, who, some folks guessed, had too much interest in the case of that murderess, Leslie Sykes. Rumor had it, Rojas worked for the Vargas family, although no one could say for certain what it was he did. That only set folks' minds less at ease, seeing how he lingered around town apparently with nothing better to do than eat and drink in the saloons, hover around the marshal's office, and have a shave or a haircut every other day at Bennett's.

That's where Rojas was the day Jessie, Ki, and the others slogged into town in the cold winter rain, leading a horse with a dead man strapped to it. Rojas' interest was certainly piqued by the sight of that ragged party, but the man who was really surprised was the hot-tempered, short-fused land baron Wilfredo Vargas.

Having left town soon after Miss Sykes was jailed for his father's murder, Vargas didn't hear the news of Jessie's return for another day. Angry as he was, he would have been pleased to learn that the dead man who Jessie and Barefoot rode into town was C.

J. Swann. Of course, he was disappointed when Rojas ascertained the corpse's identity, and Wilfredo Vargas seldom experienced disappointment without violent, lashing anger.

It seemed futile to Vargas, if not downright stupid and dangerous, to cause Jessie to disappear again— not just yet, anyway—but if Swann were still alive (and Vargas was inclined to believe he was), he would have to die. Slowly and painfully and, if Vargas could ever have his wish, repeatedly.

Barefoot was faced with a similar desire: how to prove that Wilfredo Vargas had put Swann up to the kidnapping and had put McClung and Branch up to the bushwhacking. His goal was to drill Vargas with enough lead to buy him a one-way ticket on the Deadline, but to do it legally. Not an easy proposition. So he called on Jessie to fill in some gaps and to urge her to press charges.

It was really a good enough excuse to invite the young beauty to dinner.

They arranged to meet in the Palmwood Room of the gracious Estevanico Hotel, a stately red-brick building where Austin himself, while Secretary of State in the provisional government of newly independent Texas, once stayed after the revolution. Perhaps the largest building in Sarah, the Estevanico was an imposing sight, with its classically inspired facade, its tall windows, high portico, and wrought-iron railings. Three enormous double doors opened upon a high-ceilinged lobby, where the slate floors were dressed with rich carpets, deep-cushioned chairs, and a magnificently carved mahogany front desk. Beyond the arched passage opposite a wide, curving open staircase, Barefoot sat alone in the Palmwood Room, waiting. To his wide-eyed pleasure, the lithe and feisty young Starbuck woman, who dressed in denims, riding boots, and gun belt never arrived. Instead, a curvaceous, dignified young lady in a stunning silk dress was escorted to his table by the *maître d'hôtel*. Jessie looked radiant, her lustrous honey-colored hair hanging loose over her shoulders and about her face. The emerald green of her dress accentuated her stunning green eyes, which seemed to smile as she approached. The deputy politely stood to greet her, feeling excited deep within his gut. He clenched his jaw in fear that it would hang slack with amazement, then managed to greet her without revealing his nervousness.

With a direct look, Jessie said, "I'm delighted we could find this time together." She touched Barefoot's hand, drawing every bit of his conscious attention to that one small spot where they made contact. As they took their seats Barefoot's eyes memorized every bit of Jessie's beauty: her long, curved lashes and the classical perfection of her nose; the baby-soft shoulders, exposed by the low cut of her dress; the elegant silk-strung pearl dancing above her heavenly, lush cleavage into which an iron man could readily melt. When next she smiled at him in the gentle candle light, Barefoot noticed how the bruise on her face had already faded noticeably. She would tilt her head to let her long, thick hair hide it.

Talk about her mountain ordeal didn't commence until well after their first course was served—oysters on the half-shell baked with minced spinach, garlic, and a fine cheese. They laughed when when they realized they were both moaning with pleasure with every forkful. Jessie's lips pursed when she chewed, and her eyes sometimes closed in the ecstasy of a meal that comes after tragedy.

Barefoot's respect for Jessie was heightened by her remarkable recall of events and conversations. She had plenty to say about the kidnapping and the shooting of Antonio Vargas, but ironically showed little venom regarding the theft of her bonds. She wasn't forgiving, nor was she a coward; she was confident of recovering them and determined to exact appropriate repayment from the thief.

"There's nowhere on this continent Swann can escape to safety," she said as their waiter refilled her wineglass. She thanked him and sipped. "Even if he leaves the

country, my people will turn him up sooner or later—
Oh, my!" she exclaimed.

"What is it?"

Her brow furrowed. "That wine! It's wonderful! After
a week of coffee and biscuits, this is like heaven."

"You enjoy good things," Barefoot ventured.

"I enjoy feeling good," she countered. "There is too
much in the world to make us feel bad. I like to sur-
round myself with joy. That's why I'm glad to be here
with you."

Barefoot's ears felt hot as his ego swelled.

The waiter rolled a serving truck to their tableside
and unveiled the golden stuffed pheasant Barefoot had
ordered. Decorated with its own royal plumage, the
roasted bird sat as if alive upon a silver tray, staring through sightless eyes as the waiter flambéed a
rich cognac gravy to serve over the succulent flesh a
carver sliced before them. Every new sensation, every
sight, every smell, every taste, was remarked upon,
every sip of wine and taste of food closed their eyes
in the meditation of pleasure. Jessie sopped her gravy
with a piece of bread and, without apology, sucked her
fingers clean afterward. When Barefoot smiled at her,
she withdrew one finger from her mouth more slowly,
making a quiet slurping sound as the tip came free.

"You have a good appetite," Barefoot said.

"Which appetite are you referring to?" Jessie responded.

"I've only seen how you eat."

She played with her fork on the plate. "All my appetites are very healthy, and I think they're all more or
less the same."

"What do you mean?"

"If you eat with gusto," Jessie replied, "you probably
satisfy most other appetites the same way. What about
you? Do you have strong appetites?"

"Getting stronger all the time."

"And what kind of appetites are they—besides eating?"

"The kind it takes a woman like you to satisfy."

Jessie licked gravy from her fingertip one last time. As she dried her hand with her napkin Barefoot asked, "Interested in dessert?"

"I certainly am," she said, "but what I want this place doesn't serve."

They had eaten voraciously into late evening and were growing eager to quit the hotel. An evening stroll was prevented by the chill winter mist that continued to dampen the countryside, and the hotel lounge was filled with bored travelers and some of the region's wealthy who needed to be conspicuous, although they tried desperately to seem disinterested in everything surrounding them. It was a frustrating puzzle for the couple: each wanting to be alone with the other, neither having a place to go that wouldn't be either scandalous or undesirable. Finally Jessie suggested he escort her back to Widow Pritchard's, as it was getting late. They hurried through the glossy black night, passing by Stewart's livery stable when Barefoot pointed down a small street that seemed to vanish in the dark.

"See that little clapboard down there with the white fence? That's where I'm staying. Haskins set me up. Belongs to his cousin, or some such relation."

"It's looks cozy," Jessie said. "I'd like to visit you sometime."

Barefoot faced her. "You know, Jessie, in my line of work, sometime is a might tricky thing. Ain't no telling when there's no more sometimes coming my way, if you get my meaning."

Taking his hand in her warm palm, she replied, "That's true of us all. But Sarah's a small town, Boyd, and folks all know me." She gave his hand a squeeze. "I will visit you. Soon. I want to very much."

At the door of Widow Pritchard's inn they parted, Barefoot walking backward slowly, taking in as much of this sensuous vision as possible before she slipped away, into the sliver of lamplight narrowing at the door's edge. With his hands thrust deep into his coat pockets, he sighed with disappointment and trudged back to his lonely quarters with his hands pressed against his aching abdomen.

Boyd slept soundly that night, lulled by the spirits of the evening's meal, comforted by the thick layers of blankets that protected him from the chill damp air. Across the home's only room, fingers of orange light danced from the stove grate in a fanlike pattern onto the floor, too weak to illuminate anything but the floor planks. On his bed beneath a window Barefoot slept on his stomach, dreaming it was the luscious flesh of Jessica Starbuck he pressed himself against, secure with his head covered and warm, his long black hair wild, like the tail of a horse in full gallop. Yanked suddenly from his sleep like a hooked fish being pulled from the depths, he awoke with a start, hearing what he had dreamed was screaming. His heart pounded as he listened, his wide eyes seeing nothing in the darkness. The sound came again: the distant keening of coyotes, somewhere on the outskirts of town. Their high-pitched wailing wove an eerie counterpoint, invading the dreams of all who slept in Sarah, tricking them into uncalled-for fear. Barefoot lay down again, breathing easier, and tried to sleep.

In the twilight realm between sleep and waking the sounds of gunshots startled him awake once more, bringing him bolt-upright in bed only to realize they were not gunshots at all, but knocking on his door.

"Who's there?" he shouted, lighting a candle on a table opposite his bed.

"It's me" came a faint voice. "Jessica."

Amazingly, there she stood outside the door he held open in groggy disbelief. He knew he wasn't dreaming, for no dream could be as precious as this. With arms folded, she stood huddled within her thick coat; drops of water clung to the brim of her John B. Her hair was twisted like a rope and tucked beneath her collar. Barefoot, clutching his robe closed, repeated her name and gawked as the fire in his belly was rekindled.

"Are you going to invite me in?" Jessie asked.

142

"Please!" Barefoot blurted. "Please, do!" and he stepped aside, closing the door behind her.

"I hope it's not too late for me to visit," Jessie said, removing her hat.

"Not at all," he stammered. He couldn't figure out how to phrase his question about whether Jessie was taking a chance in coming over alone at this time of night. Finally he decided it must not matter; her presence was enough. Naked beneath his robe, Barefoot held it closed with one hand while taking Jessie's coat with the other.

Jessie smiled. "Did I surprise you?"

"You might say that!" Barefoot laughed.

"Good" was Jessie's reply.

They lingered close for a year-long moment until Jessie said, "After I left you, all I could think about was seeing you again, as soon as possible. Slipping out of Pritchard's Inn is easy enough, so . . . I came over."

"I'm glad you did."

In a voice so low they could hear water dripping from the eaves outside, Jessie said, "Boyd, I . . . I'd like for you to kiss me."

Slowly, with heartbeats suspended, he drew closer. Their lips parted, and he pressed his mouth upon hers softly, tentatively. They felt the tips of each other's tongues, and he wrapped his arms around her hourglass waist, pulling her against him tightly, kissing her passionately, until their lips glistened. He felt his robe open and his pendulous member brush the front of her dress and begin to stiffen. As their embrace softened, Jessie stared deeply into Barefoot's shadowed face and breathed again. The tall deputy stepped back and drew his robe closed.

"I had to know," she whispered.

After a moment Barefoot offered to light a lantern, but she stopped him. He could see that the cold still clung to her bones.

"Care for something to drink to warm you? Tea? Pot of coffee?"

"Whiskey," she replied. "Got any?"

With a smile Barefoot said, "I'll join you."

He turned away to pour, excusing himself for not having very comfortable chairs, although his home was clean and orderly. He didn't notice the sound of many small buttons coming undone down the back of Jessie's dress as she walked toward the bed. The whiskey gurgled in the bottoms of two tin cups as silk *shushed* across cotton and slipped silently down smooth bare legs. The bottle knocked the wooden table as petticoat laces uncoiled. When Barefoot turned to bring the drinks, he saw the soft crease of Jessie's pear-shaped ass appear through the darkness, like the winter moon unveiled by parting clouds, as her petticoat fell to the floor and she stepped out of it with doe's feet. Her hair spilled down her bare back, and she knelt upon the warm bed, spreading her bottom toward the disbelieving deputy, lifted the blankets, and slipped into bed. Barefoot's heart was like a sledgehammer against his chest. He stepped closer, feeling the heaviness of his genitals swaying free of the open robe.

"How's your appetite tonight, Boyd?"

"Starving."

He stood beside the bed and offered her a cup. She reached out . . . and ran her hand up the inside of his thigh, higher until she brushed the hair at the bottom of his balls. A thrill rose through his central nerve. Like a feather, her hand drew down the length of his penis and through his pubic hair. She cupped the growing flesh in her palm and curled her fingers around it, pulling it gently until she heard Barefoot's first groan of pleasure. Then she gripped more firmly and began stroking in earnest, bringing him to a mighty erection, an immediate response to long neglect.

Jessie rose upon one elbow and pressed her face against the hot, veined flesh. She held it against her cheeks, her lips, her neck. She sat up, never releasing her warm, light grip. Her other hand touched his thigh and fingertips danced up the back of his leg, igniting sparks of excitement that propelled his pelvis forward and back. Her lips parted. She pursed them over the tip of his cock and with her tongue brushed and poked the small opening. Then, moving her grip to the very base of his erection, she clamped her soft, thick lips around it and slowly moved forward, swallowing the great shaft inch by teasing inch until he felt his glans poke the back of her throat; yet still she swallowed, ramming his turgid flesh into herself until her lips touched her hand and her breath was felt in his hair.

She pulled away with a *slurp* and, gripping the base of his huge swollen cock, began sucking hungrily, thrusting up and down more violently with every moan of approval from Barefoot, finally humming with delight herself. She took him in to the hilt once again, and Barefoot's groan was nearly a roar when she pulled herself away.

She gasped, "You always this hard, or you just ain't been getting it lately?"

"Been a long time, all right," he said, "but I ain't never had it this good."

Jessie chuckled and said, "Maybe we should have those drinks before we get too carried away."

"Don't stop now!" Barefoot whined.

"Don't worry. I won't let you down. Come on, get in bed."

They toasted Jessie's safe return to Sarah, musing on the miracle of their being together. The single candle imbued them with a rich golden glow that made Jessie's face and hair even more radiant. Her plush, shining lips were moist and willing, and Barefoot impetuously kissed her repeatedly, deeply, feeling her adventurous tongue cooled by the volatile drink.

She dipped a finger into her cup and dabbed the cold fluid on Barefoot's nipples. She leaned over and licked them clean like a mother lioness, then teased them like a seductress. She sucked them while exploring his groin with one hand, softly rubbing her palm from below his balls up the length of his pulsating shaft. He could take it no longer.

He placed the cups on the floor. His hands caressed her luscious breasts, teasing her nipples to large, pink erections that he took between his lips and suckled. He pulled and stretched them while sliding one hand behind her and kneading her buttock. They kissed again, and Jessie pressed her primed vulva against Barefoot's thigh, smearing it with hot, smooth fluid. Reaching between the crescent of her ass, he found her honeyed inner lips and massaged them, smearing them with her natural juices, plunging into her hot love canal with one, two, then three fingers. Jessie writhed and kissed him more strongly. She reached down and placed the head of his cock against her firm clitoris, rubbing it back and forth and raising her leg higher to expose her needful sex.

She rolled him onto his back, and raising one leg, she turned and straddled his head, bringing her gaping, wet pussy down upon his face for him to devour. On one knee and with one leg raised, she rocked her pelvis over his mouth, voicing her pleasure each time Barefoot's tongue pierced her. She leaned forward, placing her clitoris well between his lips, and lifted his reclining cock to her mouth, opening wide to wrap her lips around his engorged purple head. Pulling him into her mouth, Jessie sucked and shook her head wildly. She stretched the skin back taut and alternated between oscillating her head upon it and driving it deep into her throat for a prolonged, penetrating thrust. Barefoot responded by stretching her labia wide open, burying his nose into the moist, pink folds of her musky vagina while sucking her bulging pearl like a baby at the tit. As they rocked and thrust, Jessie's full breasts and large, darkened nipples rubbed his stomach. When Barefoot's moaning became rapid, on the verge of losing control, Jessie tightened her grip at the base of his prick and slowed her torrid pace. At that point Barefoot rolled her over and turned to mount her from above.

She lay on her back and held her knees up beside her breasts. Barefoot knelt before her and rubbed her clitoris with the head of his penis, inserting it in her flowing vagina and removing it, again and again. Leaning back, he retrieved a pillow, lifted Jessie's well-licked ass, and placed it beneath. The sumptuous feast of her sex, enmeshed within a thicket of copper-blond pubic hair, lay exposed and waiting. His long, sleek black hair hung in front of his shoulders, enshrouding his face. His breath was heavy.

"You are so beautiful," he whispered. "I can't believe how beautiful."

"I want you inside me," said Jessie.

He leaned over and, with a slow, steady, nearly downward thrust, plunged deep into her belly until he felt his balls against her ass. Withdrawing almost completely, he plunged again and repeated his taunting while Jessie watched the bold thickness of him disappear into her wet, hairy cleavage. She reached behind herself to find his scrotum and held him behind the balls so that with every withdrawal, his sac stretched and pulled him back into her. She clenched two fingers around the root of his slippery penis and squeezed, hardening his erection still further and bringing his thrusting to a peak of passion. When he pressed himself into her as far as he could go and held himself there, Jessie flexed little-known muscles within her love-slick pussy and squeezed his cock in the most intoxicating ways.

Jessie gritted her teeth. She embraced his shoulders. She closed her legs around him and locked her feet together, buying leverage with which to screw her hips with cock-bending skill. She had learned well the ancient arts of love revealed to her by her father's Japanese housekeeper and now lived in a balance that made love as powerful as work and fighting to survive. Unraveling her feet, she dug her heels into Barefoot's pumping backside like spurs into a stallion. Her toes flared in lusty delirium as she drove him deeper into herself, one heel galvanizing his frenzy by pressing into the softness between his buttocks. Beads of sweat twinkled like diamond facets on his face and chest, and the candlelight threw his long-haired rocking shadow across the wall and window behind. Clutching his head to her shoulder, Jessie felt Barefoot's thrusts grow more insistent. The head of his penis grew enormous and rock-hard, his breathing became stormy, and he sweated profusely. He yelled and rose up on his hands, plowing his pelvis in a relentless rampage until he yelled once again as the first copious jet of white-hot cum spewed from the very root of his being. He yelled again as the spasms of orgasm weakened his spine, and yelled one last time as a windowpane and the shadowed shade behind him exploded, pitching splintered glass into the bed following two terrifying close-together blasts. Barefoot's forehead shattered into a halo of thick, dark blood and bone as his back arched with the other impact, and though he died instantly, his involuntary ejaculations into the screaming woman below continued even after she pulled herself free of him.

★

Chapter 13

Stifling her mad hollering, the terrified woman threw herself to the floor just as two more bullets burst through the glass and shade and bored into the opposite wall. Her thoughts flew to her coat—her twin-barrel .38 derringer was in its pocket—but then she remembered seeing a brace of pistols hanging in a gun belt on the wall. Wiping Barefoot's blood from her face, she skittered across the floor when another brief fusillade shattered the silence. Jessie found a boot and threw it at the candle. When it hit the floor, she scrambled over to blow it out, then bolted for the pistols. Pulling his Smith & Wesson from the leather, she checked the cylinder and crabbed to another window, staying well below the sill.

The heat of her interrupted passion was vanishing; her bare skin turned to gooseflesh with cold fear as she peeked out the window, unable to see anything in the blackness. Thick blood spattered her chest and smeared her face. She flinched with the next gun blast, but the flash gave away the gunner's position. Another muzzle flash showed him to be high and on the move, probably on horseback, probably wielding a rifle. Gripping the pistol with two hands, Jessie squeezed off four rapid shots through the glass, in a wide spray, then rolled away, across the floor. She heard a guttural curse in a demonic voice she had grown to know too well to mistaken. As she clambered onto the bed before the other window, reloading for another volley, the rataplan of hooves receded into the deep Texas night. Naked, chilled, on the verge of tears, Jessie looked at the tragedy before her and stroked her forehead in grief.

Before any townsfolk appeared in the wake of the sudden violence, she was dressed and heading for the inn. She wondered if Ki would be as amazed as she was by Swann's stupidity for not having put Sarah far behind him, but she didn't have to wonder long. Ever vigilant, Ki had known all along where she had gone since he heard her slipping out of her room. He had *haragei*—a gut sense—for danger that seemed to project far beyond his body and his physical surroundings. Sleeping half dressed, he was out the door so soon after the first gunshot sounded that Widow Pritchard feared for her own life and for her guests', thinking that the disturbance was right within her own home. From within the building Ki could distinguish the sound of two different weapons, one of them, Jessie's, sounding muffled due to the indoor discharges. Now, fearing the worst, moving as swiftly and as gracefully as a lean-muscled buck on the run, he knifed through the cold night air toward the disturbance and met Jessie halfway.

"That son of a bitch is back!" she yelled frantically. "He murdered Boyd."

Ki held her by her shoulders, straining to see her face in the dark. The dark droplets clinging in the wells of her eyes and lining the creases in her brow startled him.

"Are you all right? Are you hurt?"

"He's alive!" Jessie panted. "The insane bastard's alive!"

"Who, Jessie? What are you saying?"

"Swann!"

"Alive?" Ki became flustered trying to sort the story of Swann's death after he attacked Jessie. Jessie put off explaining in favor of insisting that Swann had tried to kill her once again and that he was on the run. Ki pulled her by the hand, spitting out plans for pursuit, saying, "Let's go!" as Jessie tried to keep up.

"You can't follow him in the dark" she protested. "He's gone! It's dark!"

"Like hell I can't! I got a hunch he's headed back to the only place he's ever felt safe. Come on! We're riding out. Now!"

It was still hours before dawn, but Ki led Jessie on a hell-bent ride through the brittle, cold-forged night on horses spooked by the predawn haste. She rode Barefoot's dun gelding; Ki, Judd's sturdy dapple—two desperate hunters riding the mounts of dead men. Alone together, they raced away from where the sun would soon rise, toward the harsh mountain fastness that the warmth of day would again forsake, a chain of broken earth which even now, in dismal sunlessness, loomed a pale, deathly white above the horizon, like a host of lost spirits bound to the earth.

In his furious pace, more than once Ki lost his forward momentum and, reining the responsive dapple into sudden, meandering turns, backtracked and searched desperately for some sign of Swann's route, some reminder of the short path back to the killing grounds high in the saw-toothed ridges of the Diablos. At first Jessie's fear was curtailed by Ki's quick and sure resumption of the chase, but soon she questioned the wisdom of tracking blindly aloud.

Ki responded heatedly, insisting they continue no matter what may happen. This was Ki, a decided leaning toward fiery response, sudden, hard action, even anger. Without realizing it, Jessie stood in stark contrast to her longtime friend and protector. She was blessed—Ki, himself, would say "skilled"—with a certain restraint that balanced lightning reaction with

151

earthy confidence and oceanic vigilance. Although in the aftermath of the night's terror she was comfortable letting Ki choose the way, and though fear rode her as if she were a quarter horse, she forged ahead. Trust and anger drew her on.

"Oh, Lawd a'mighty!" intoned the horrified dry goods store owner, Whittaker. He was the first person to enter Barefoot's cottage after the shooting stopped. He was followed immediately by John Stewart, the livery owner, who lived two lots down. He in turn enlisted the next man to appear to stand outside to prevent others from crowding into the house. In the light of the lantern he was carrying, Whittaker grimaced at the sight of the once handsome young deputy sprawled naked across the bed, the top third of his face missing. A small river of blood also issued from a blackened hole between the dead man's shoulder blades.

"Should we get the doctor?" Stewart asked.

"Ain't no rush, John, except to sign the papers. This boy's about as gone as the year before last." He deplored the murder with a curse and asked Stewart to help see what could be found.

The pistol Jessie had fired still lay upon the bed, fully loaded, beneath the ruined window. Whittaker lifted the barrel to his nose and sniffed. His mustache hid his frown. As he placed the gun down he kicked something beneath the bed—one of the two tin cups. He lifted one. There was still some whiskey in it.

"Reckon Boyd had a guest," Stewart said.

Whittaker grunted in affirmation. "Whoever it was done threw some lead back at the man who ambushed them, I'd venture."

"How d'you figger?"

"Gun's been fired and reloaded, and Boyd's facing the wrong way to be shooting out the window when he got hit."

Stewart harrumphed and walked around the bed to look at the front of Barefoot's body. He made an effort to keep his eyes from Barefoot's face.

"Poor bastard was caught at a awkward time, I'd say." He waved one hand in the direction of Barefoot's crotch. Whittaker looked over and saw the dollops of ivory jism on the pillow beneath the deputy's pelvis and a single glassy string dripping from his penis. The pubic hair and chest hair were matted with moisture.

Whittaker clicked his tongue. With a sympathetic tone, "Let's just cover him up, John. Maybe tell the doc. Ain't nobody else need to know such things. He was a good man, best I could tell. And there sure are worse ways to die."

As he headed for the door again, Steward glanced down at the table by the wall, where he saw several small slips of paper lying beneath a pocket watch. He lifted them to read the writing.

"Hey, Whit, whaddya make of this?"

Whittaker took a close look at the handwriting and read it aloud: " *'Vargas owes Dupree $8.50 from Tatum's share'*? This one's for five bucks, this one's six . . ." His forehead furrowed when he looked at Stewart. "It's a mark awright, prob'ly a poker debt. I seen plenty."

"With Vargas's name on it? And Dupree—ain't that the name of the guy Miss Starbuck rode in, the one who caught lead?"

Whittacker stroked his mustache and said, "Yeah. . . . I'll bet a double eagle ol' Boyd here was onto somethin'."

Daybreak in the foothills was a spectacular display of limitless sky, streaked with high mare's tails that relinquished their midnight gloom for the blush of morning and then for the white of a long day to come. Likewise, the snowy landscape no longer glowed with a pale moonlike coolness. As the skies brightened, the snow cover turned pale blue and grew stark white, despite the mountain shadows. Agaves stubbornly held their burdens of snow upon their stiff, spiny arms, refusing to bend. Pine-firs, heavy with snow, and madrones, shedding their paper-thin bark, stood like paintings in the still air. A sinuous V of wintering snow geese lithely flew toward the sun, their black-tipped wings becoming all that was visible before they vanished, honking without care, into white. The grandeur of the dawn was lost upon the riders, who hurried back into the grip of winter. all the returning light brought them was quicker pace, sharper eyes, and faster won progress.

Swann had come this way many a time throughout his gun-wild life, especially since crossing paths with the Vargas family, and he knew the lay of the land. Although darkness had slowed him considerably, he proceeded steadily. By midmorning he was nearing the familiar final passages toward his oft-used mountain lair—the almost treeless valley above the loud-rushing stream, the footbridge across it and into the cut, the copse of trees where he had camped not long ago. It occurred to him that after years of taking refuge from the law in this lonely mountain realm, its whereabouts had finally been revealed, compromised, and it was no longer much good to him. He had done what he swore he would do: kill the troublesome Jessica Starbuck. Blew her into kingdom come without even getting off his horse, the lucky result of a thoughtlessly placed candle that threw her long-haired shadow across the shaded window. His success didn't come without its price. He cursed the dumb-ass deputy who fired back, grazing Swann's calf as his horse turned toward the leaving side of town. A lucky shot for the cockeyed lawman; a searing, bloody mess for Swann, for whom pain was but a good reason to get even. That was the lesson he felt he had taught the "Starbuck bitch."

Now he had another goal in mind: retrieve the bonds he had hidden and vamoose. He figured he'd cash the bonds in El Paso, then vanish forever, no one would know in which direction. Maybe he'd find some down-at-the-heels hoot owl in need of a drinking partner, get him mindlessly drunk, then shave half his head, put a crucifix around his neck, and leave him wondering why the Texas Rangers were shooting at him. He'd buy a stage fare north to Santa Fe and miss its departure.

After that, it would be anyone's guess which way the man who stole the Starbuck fortune went. He knew the right people in Ciudad Juárez—businessmen who worked a lively trade between the bluecoats at Fort Bliss and local Mimbrenos in need of arms—people who could get him to Bisbee from just south of the border, with little trouble from either General Trevino's easily bought garrisons or Victorio's marauders. He lusted for the fallen angels to be found in Palomas or Ascensión, senoritas who would do anything at all for the price of a meal. He rubbed his crotch in anticipation. He entertained grand visions of making some of the silver mines around Bisbee and Tombstone his own, then moving on once more, toward the Pacific coast around Ensenada. Not a bad place, he thought, for a filthy-rich American to pass his final days like a king.

He crested the rise above the gorge. The steep-walled streambed was still bathed in misty shadow. The loneliness of the place made Swann feel free. He gave his plans more thought before crossing the bridge, where he dismounted to urinate. Stepping down from the stirrup, his grazed leg flared with a pain like deep smoldering fire. His pant leg was more blood-soaked than he had thought, and his boot was slick with it, leaving red marks in the virgin-white snow. He tried to walk on it awhile, strolling down the embankment at the mouth of the gorge to stretch himself. A few feet above the stream he yellowed the snow, then climbed stiffly back to his broomtail.

Quickly putting the bridge behind him, he maintained a quick pace beyond the copse of trees, and rounding the final slope approaching the cabin, he yanked his mount to a halt and froze at the sight before him.

Two fully rigged horses were hitched to the post at the side of the cabin. Someone was inside. For the first time, he was thankful for the snow which disguised the sound of hoofs. He looked for a place to hide until he knew what he was up against—until he knew who was in the cabin and why. The hill behind the cabin was too steep to negotiate in snow, so he kneed the animal up the opposite slope, toward a stand of trees lining the ridge. The going was treacherous. He turned the horse into ascending switchbacks when possible, all the while keeping a nervous eye on the cabin. Its bare window was his greatest threat. In the still air he could hear his own breathing amid the labored respiration of the horse and the scrunch of snow.

The tree line was only yards away. He had nudged the beast around a sapling when two powerful shots thundered through the valley. Swann's horse flinched with a pained whine. Another shot punched the animal hard in the chest, sending it and its rider toppling downhill, screaming. Swann came clear of the saddle and slid deep into several feet of snow. He tried to come to his feet while avoiding the flailing broomtail. Sitting up, he drew his revolver and scanned the hillside as two men stepped from the cabin below. Before Swann could find the gunman, another shot rang out, piercing his cuff.

"Drop it!" shouted a crouching man from behind a nearby tree. To his shoulder he held a Winchester. Farther back in the stand was his mount, hitched to a tree branch. "I'll blow you to hell right now if you don't drop it!"

The gun flipped from Swann's hand and disappeared in the snow. "All right!" Swann yelled. "Don't shoot!"

"Get up!" He ordered Swann away from the horse as he approached. "Hey!" he yelled to the men downhill, "I got him!"

When Swann was safely away from the wounded animal, the gunman stepped closer to it, quickly jerked the rifle toward the animal, and shot it through the head. "This way," he ordered, leading Swann uphill so he could retrieve his horse.

With the rifle at his back Swann slipped and slid down to the cabin, his wounded leg throbbing like a steam engine. He was cold and bruised, and he schemed for a way to turn the tables on his captor. The two men at the cabin door waited confidently. Nearing the bottom of the hill, Swann recognized the shorter, dark-skinned man: Rojas, the contemptuous buzzard who never got his fill of tormenting him. The man next to him held a pistol.

"*Hola, amigo!*" hailed Rojas. "I spect you come here." He took a step closer, coming face to face with Swann, and with blurring speed threw a fist that made Swann stagger. Swann's attempted retaliation was prevented by two gun barrels, forward and behind, and one huge hand clutching the lapels of his coat.

Shaking his smarting fist, Rojas sneered, "You filthy dog, you tell me you do what we ask you. *Pero no*. You turn everything up and down. *Idiota, estupido*. You are shit in the desert. A woman with nothing between her legs."

Just then Swann noticed something dark lying partially covered in snow by the side of the cabin. He looked harder and saw a bloodied human hand and the sole of a boot.

Following his eyes, Rojas said, "You know this man, *si*? We find him inside. Something very bad happen to him."

"Name's Tatum," Swann grumbled.

"You kill him so you no haff to pay him, *si*?"

"We had a fight and—"

"He die, more *pesos* for you!"

"He stole my whiskey. I had to—"

"No. You no kill a man for whiskey, you kill for something else."

"Listen, you greasy, bean-eating runt, I killed him because—"

The Mexican's fist snapped forward, pummeling Swann in the stomach. He grabbed the back of his head and drove his face into his raised knee, then tried to punch him across the side of the head, but Swann lunged. He hit the smaller man in the midsection with his shoulder, pounding him against the cabin wall, but that was as far as it went before the *pistolero* whipped him from behind and dropped him to his knees. As a parting gesture, Rojas booted him squarely in mouth, spewing blood into the snow where Swann fell to his elbows.

Rojas railed at him, with veins bulging in his forehead. "You let the woman escape! You kill the men who help you! Now you try to run and hide! I want to know why before I kill you, too!"

Swann held his throbbing jaw as blood from his teeth and nose trickled between his fingers. He tried to sit upright. Rojas put his hand out to the man holding the Winchester and said, "*Da me*." Taking the rifle by the barrel, he lifted it above his shoulder and said, "Talk!" With a sudden *whoosh*, the Winchester came down across Swann's back and the valley echoed with his bellow. "*Digame*," Rojas said. "Why you let Starbuck woman escape?"

"I don't know what you're talking about!" Swann mumbled. "I killed her. I shot her myself, in town last night!"

Furiously Rojas shook him by his coat lapels, screaming, "She was at the stables after the marshal was shot!"

"Marshal?" The shadow on the shaded window was a woman's, he was sure of it.

Swann's eyes seemed to swell with surprise as he listened to Rojas repeat the news. Rojas derided him for trying to kill the woman after he had been instructed not to harm her. Handing the rifle back to his gun hawk, he drew a gleaming double-edged blade from a sheath beneath his coat. Its handle was wrapped with the skin of a rattler. Stepping behind his addled victim, he grabbed a handful of Swann's hair and jerked his head back. The razor-edged steel came to his throat.

"This will give me great pleasure, *Señor* Swann. All the blood in your body will squirt out, *pero*, little by little. You will feel very, very cold, and you will take a very long time to die. And I will stand here so you can watch me laugh at you. *Adios!*"

158

"Rojas, wait!" Swann gasped. "I killed Tatum for the money the woman had. Thousands of dollars, American, Rojas, in a pair of saddlebags. I swear!"

"*Si*, and I have a brain as small as yours. Good-bye, dog."

Swann squirmed. "In the cabin! I swear! You're gonna kill me if it ain't true, but it is! I can pay Vargas everything I owe him and more. I can pay you more than you'll see in three lifetimes. Ten thousand dollars in negotiable bonds!"

The blade hovered. A glimmer of hope filled Swann's pounding heart.

"That's why I killed Tatum," he continued. "He tried to steal it all and not take a share. That's why I had to try to kill the woman. She knew too much about me. She had the bonds when we ambushed her on the road. I swear on my life it's true, Rojas, and you can have a share, the largest share. I can get square with Vargas, and you'll never have to see my face again. Don't kill me before you find out the truth!"

Rojas wavered. He couldn't trust the ugly bandito anymore than he could fly, but there was really nothing to lose; Swann would die either way, bonds or no bonds. Injured, unarmed, and desperate, Swann posed no real threat. Deep down, he was just a sniveling coward.

"In the cabin, you say?"

Swann nodded. "Under a cot, under the floorboards."

The blade withdrew, and Rojas released Swann's hair. They ordered him to his feet and to produce the bonds. He limped into the demolished room and pointed demurely toward the cot Jessie had slept upon.

"It's under here," he said.

After a moment's thought, Rojas ordered him to get it. Swann fell to his knees and stuck his head under the cot.

"There are two guns pointed right at your *culo*, Swann. If you try anything, one of us is sure to kill you."

"You wouldn't shoot me in the ass now, would you, Rojas?"

The swarthy knifeman sneered, "Only a coward thinks all men are cowards like him."

Squatting down for a better view, Rojas watched Swann pry a floorboard loose and turn it over. He lifted a second one and roughly worked a leather bag from the hole within.

"I hid it under here before going back to town, just in case I got hung up," Swann grunted. He backed out from under the cot and struggled to his feet. He pointed to the deep gash in the side of his head left by Jessie's gunshot. "Look at this. That bitch did that. Knocked me out cold, and when I woke up, she was gone. Left me for dead."

"Shut up and give me the bag," Rojas demanded.

Swann continued, "Bitch was stupid enough to leave me a horse, so I ran her down and got this before the deputy showed up."

"*Da me!*" Rojas seized one side of the saddlebag and undid the buckle while Swann, holding the other half, worked the other side. The Mexican drew a breath of genuine astonishment. "*Aye, dios mio!*" he said, pulling out a handful of the bonds, bedazzled by the truth of Swann's promise. The gun hawks were visibly shaken.

Throwing open the other flap, Swann exclaimed, "And look! There's even more!"

He thrust one arm into the bag, took hold of Dupree's Remington he had stashed there, stomped his foot to disguise the sound of the hammer cocking, and blew a hole in the face of the astounded rifleman, from inside the leather. Instantly he cleared the bag and fanned off a second shot at the *pistolero,* hitting him high in the chest. The saddlebag went down; Rojas reached for his blade. Swann tried to cock the pistol, but the rattlesnake-fast knifeman slashed him across the wrist too soon.

Nearly dropping the Remington, Swann backed off from a deadly lunge to his ribs. With a sweeping backhand motion, he bashed him with the grip of the pistol, tumbling him to his knee. Swann cocked the gun

160

and turned. Rojas kicked his legs out from under him, bringing him down hard on the edge of the cot. He kicked Swann in the face with his heel as he turned the knife downward in his hand. With an arcing swing, he jabbed down on Swann's gun hand, piercing it between two fingers, clear through to the pistol grip. With the howl of a hound from hell, Swann lost the gun.

Rojas kicked it out of reach and brought his blade down a second time, but Swann caught his arm when the steel spike was only inches from his ribs. He tried to twist the powerful arm away with his good hand, but left his face open to attack. Rojas's lightning fist hammered the bridge of his nose, numbing his head and firing Swann's anger with renewed strength.

He rolled away as Rojas's razor edge skimmed past his face. Seizing the nearest cot, Swann turned it on top of his enraged opponent and leaped for the Winchester, unaware that Rojas, far stronger than his small stature would suggest, had heaved the entire wooden cot into the air. As Swann reached for the weapon he was flattened to the floor, with the cot on top of him. Rojas pounced like a polecat, leaping upon the cot as Swann struggled beneath it and jabbing at him with his blade. A great, bloodcurdling yawp went up when the steel penetrated Swann's thigh. Driven wild with rage, Swann reached for Rojas's leg, clamped his arm behind his knee, and pushed against the cot, simultaneously pulling Rojas's leg toward him. The entire bed tumbled over, throwing Rojas to the floor, near the stove.

Lifting the Winchester, Swann leveled it to fire, only to see the flash of spinning steel snicking through the air. He jerked the barrel to the side and flinched, hearing the clatter of steel against steel as the blade was deflected. From beneath the wood stove Rojas pulled the iron poker and sprung to his feet. He swung as the Winchester's smoke hole closed upon him and slammed the barrel away as the weapon deafeningly discharged. He lunged to get behind the muzzle, driving the poker like a spear, but Swann repelled it. Without breaking stride, Rojas threw a pulverizing elbow to his brow and clamped a powerful hand around Swann's knotty throat. Swann's groaning became squelched as he crushed down mightily on his trachea.

Together they fell back, across the hard edge of the overturned table, Rojas taking the rib-snapping fall worse. The poker clattered to the floor. His choke hold came loose, and Swann backhanded him across the face with calloused knuckles. He grabbed Rojas by the ears and plunged his thumbs hard into his eyes. The swarthy man sputtered in agony. He raked Swann's face with jagged fingernails, but Swann held fast. He clawed at his mouth, trying to tear lips from the bone, but still Swann bore down. He moved one hand blindly across the littered floor, found something sharp—a shard of glass. He gripped it hard enough to draw his own blood and jabbed for Swann's neck, gouging him badly across the jaw and breaking Swann's eyebursting hold. Unable to see, Rojas swiped the air with the glass, spraying the room with blood.

Seeing his chance, Swann took Rojas by his coat and tried to thrash him against the stove, several feet away, but the little man was swift. With chilling accuracy, he sent a fist into a pendulum arc, nailing Swann in the testes and putting him down on his back, beside a toppled chair. Rojas found his knife, gripped it point down, and fell upon his numbed adversary, aiming to gut him, but Swann pulled the chair over himself, catching Rojas's arm once again at a safe distance. With two hands he held the knife-wielding wrist and pulled Rojas down into a sideways tumble that threw him over the wounded *pistolero*.

Rojas landed upon the revolver. Swann fell back for the poker. The hammer of the gun caught on Rojas's clothing, and he fought to free it while the poker rose in a backswing. He raised the weapon as Swann sickled the air. The hammer pulled back, but the flailing poker made contact before the firing pin was struck. The explosive blast came almost on top of the crack of bone, just late enough to send the slug astray, past Swann's shoulder. With a barbaric yell of triumph Swann brought the poker down again, like a highswung battle-ax, and cleaved the jaw of his opponent wide open, filling his mouth with jagged bits of shattered teeth. Raving savagely, he swung repeatedly, mutilating the face and head of the supine man, cursing and damning him for every past wrong, continuing the withering, insane bludgeoning in rhythm to his shouts and animal grunts, reddening the soot-gray ceiling with each infuriated swipe. When finally he exhausted himself, he continued to curse Rojas breathlessly as he casually lifted the Winchester and, holding it with his one good hand, levered shot after shot into the gelatinous mess that was once a man. He turned the weapon upon the wounded *pistolero* and triggered a disappointing click, having already spent his last cartridge. He looked with conquering pride over the room and spat upon each of the Vargas men out of blood-simple triumph, out of spite, out of a desire to flaunt his utter defiance of the most arrogant land baron in West Texas.

Retrieving the saddlebag, he crouched to collect the bonds. Some were blood-spattered, others were soaked in it. He absently wiped them on whatever presented itself—blanket, mattress, Rojas's coat sleeve—and stuffed them haphazardly into the bag. Seizing one good gun, he opened the door, flooding the grisly scene with brilliant white light. Looking over his insane handiwork, he cried out in a brittle choked roar, "Fuck you all!" and slammed the door behind him as hard as he could.

★

Chapter 14

The occasional coin-sized spots of red in the snow along Swann's trail didn't escape Ki's sharp eyes. They became larger and more noticeable as the trail dragged on, telling Ki that Swann's wound was bad enough for the blood to soak his clothing and run off. Since daylight he and Jessie spurred their mounts forward at a grueling pace, closing the gap between themselves and their quarry more every mile. Before long they were in familiar country, with not far to go to the cabin. They proceeded as cautiously as possible.

Ki figured the mountains were Swann's safest escape and that Swann probably had supplies and horses cached at the cabin or nearby. He suspected Swann would head due south after quitting the Sierra Diablos, through the less defended terrain between forts Quitman and Davis. He didn't realize how brazen Swann truly was, that the scar-headed demon would have no reluctance to pass directly through the string of army outposts along the Rio Grande frontier, stretching north from Fort Bliss, near El Paso. One thing Ki felt sure of: unless they made better time than Swann, there'd be no finding him in Texas.

Swann was thinking to himself as he crested the saddle of land overlooking the high side of the gorge, *I think I'll send Vargas a letter from Juárez and thank him for everything.* Just then, looking through the angled walls of the cut, he saw two riders on the distant hill, heading for the bridge. He cursed out loud and veered wide to stay among the trees, out of sight. Following the path he had taken earlier to the top of the cut, he came to a point just above the trees where he could look out upon the mouth of the gorge. He recognized the riders.

That prick Rojas was right, he thought. *Starbuck's alive.* He recognized Ki as the man he had shot during the ambush and said aloud, "Guess me and him ain't the dying kind. We'll see about that." Moving quietly was no problem in the snow. He started the descent into the cut.

Seeing nothing amiss, Jessie and Ki came to the mouth of the gorge, keeping an eye on the ridge tops above. They were about to proceed across the bridge when Ki said, "Hold it!" and pointed down at the trampled snow painted with smatterings of red. Shoe prints trailed off along the narrow embankment upstream, into the gorge. Ki drew his pistol and said, "I'm going in. Stay alert."

"You don't think Swann's stupid enough to hide out in a box and leave a trail besides, do you?"

"No," said Ki, "but we don't know what he may have hid in there. Be right back."

He moved slowly along, careful to keep his mount on the most level ground possible. Jessie, meanwhile, had thoughts of her own.

Behind them, uphill, they had passed the horse Ki had to put down after Swann wounded it, and ahead, just feet from the tree line within the cut, lay Jessie's handsome steeldust that Swann had slaughtered. It was impossible to have carried the horses' rigging back with them last time with so few animals. Intent upon ultimately retrieving her embossed saddle with the silver conchas, Jessie was curious about the gear's condition after several days in the snow. She rode across the bridge and dismounted well beyond the fallen steeldust, hiding the dun in a copse at the foot of the canyon wall. Fortunately, she found the cold weather had prevented the snow from melting on the saddle beyond what the body heat of the dying animal did.

She started undoing the double cinch. There was some blood in the embossing on the skirt. With her thumbnail, she scraped it off, then tried to pull the blanket from beneath the saddle. She was startled by the sudden flight of two mourning doves from the trees high above. They didn't fly away smoothly, but appeared frightened. She crouched lower, peering through the trees. At the most distant point she could see through the foliage, something moved, looking like the legs of a horse, and her heart raced.

She scrambled toward her mount. At the opening of the cut above the steep embankment, there was a huge rock with the trunk of a great old tree lying across it, and she ducked into the shadow behind them, working her way uphill for a better view. She drew her slate-gray Colt .38 and checked the cylinder. Looking back across the stream, she could see no sign of Ki. She held her breath.

Swann's next view of the bridge puzzled him. He had descended along the cliff face leading down into the cut, following a small channel that fed into the main drainage gully. Beside a large spur in the wall he paused for a look. Where before he had seen two horses, now there was only one, without a rider. Since Jessie and Ki had separated, he figured it was imperative to find out where they were before they discovered him. The spur by which he stood was deep enough to conceal his mount, so he tethered the beast there and carefully started downhill. From a deep pocket in his long black coat, he drew his Russian.

Ki followed the bloody footprints far enough to realize there was nothing to be found. The yellow stains in the snow beside the river were not the end of the prints, but where they doubled back toward the bridge there was no sign of otherwise disturbed snow cover. Nothing buried, nothing hidden. He started back to his horse.

From where Jessie lay in her blind, she could see nothing of the river. Had she not been so low to the ground, she still wouldn't have been able to see her partner, who was walking outside the narrow line of sight which the cut allowed. Without knowing it, this was to her advantage, for she soon heard the soft scrunching of footsteps in the snow as Swann, unaware of how close his female adversary now was, continued down into the narrowing ravine.

Jessie crooked her elbow around her mouth and nose to prevent her visible breath from rising. Except for Swann's footsteps, the silence was total. Lowering her head to the snow, she could peer through the thin horizontal slit beneath the tree trunk. Just a few feet away, she saw the familiar trouser legs and boots of C. J. Swann move past. Her heart beat so heavily she feared he would hear it. Though she lay perfectly still on the snow-covered ground, beads of sweat rose upon her brow. To her right a tiny scurrying sound made her flinch, the motion of a lone mockingbird just discovering her presence.

She waited breathlessly. What seemed like hours passed before she could no longer hear Swann's movements. She craned her head down lower, trying to see downhill from her secret vantage point, but her view was obstructed. Still she waited.

Finally she would move. Without rising, she first observed her enclosure carefully. Finding a tangle of branches that would conceal her best while she looked over the tree trunk, she moved, like a stalking cat, to a sitting position. The Colt came up with her. She looked over. There was no trace of Swann, but across the gully she spied his mount. To her excitement her fine leather saddlebags were slung behind the cantle. She glanced downhill once again. No Swann.

Skulking low, she creeped out of her blind and silently made her way to the bay. She came upon it in plain sight, and the animal made no commotion. A strengthening wind rattled the tree branches and froze her momentarily in her tracks. She took advantage of the noise, as cover for her own movements. Flipping the strap from the buckle, she pulled the bag open and caught her breath at the sight of her bonds stuffed inside, apparently secure.

Swann stopped between two thickly branching trees just yards below her, around an obscuring curve in the canyon wall, and considered his next moves. He had come down to the opening of the cut at the top of the stream bank. From there he thought he saw movement in the bushes opposite, not far from the lone gelding. There was no sign of the woman, and that worried him. He didn't like leaving the bonds out of his sight, so he turned back and headed for his horse, keeping low in the ravine beside the sheer rock wall.

The wind gusted with a sound like a waterfall, allowing Jessie to slip the bags from the horse's back, without fear. The dangling buckle jingled against the supple hide, and she clapped her hand over it to silence it. With the bag in one arm she crept back toward her blind.

Stealthily she went, keeping her eyes peeled for Swann and shooting glances at the uneven ground, choosing each footfall with care. The scrunch of the snow seemed deafening to her fearful ears. At the edge of the main channel she paused. The way back to the blind was rugged; it was luck that had kept her from slipping the first time. She changed course, heading for the downhill side of the blind: if Swann spotted her, she wouldn't be far from cover; if not, she'd make for the dun. She stepped forward.

Something skittered across the snow uphill from her. In her peripheral vision she only saw a blur and heard the noise. She spun, brandishing the Colt, ready to fire at the large hare she had flushed as it streaked noisily into the brush. She spun again: there was Swann stepping uphill, aiming his Russian right at her.

She dove for cover, but slipped mid-lunge at the moment of the blast, again a stroke of luck, for Swann was leading his shot. *Spang!* went the bullet off the huge rock, right where Jessie would have been, had she accomplished the leap she intended.

"Ki-i-i-i!" she screamed with a face full of snow. She rolled and triggered two shots in close succession. Swann dropped for cover, and she scrambled on her belly toward the rock. Swann sprung upon her like a mountain lion. With the Russian pointed at the back of her head, he clamped one hand on her collar and turned her over. He snapped a viselike grip on her gun hand and put a knee on her chest, turning the double-action downward toward her eyes. She saw his grip tighten.

"You think you're too damn good for a no-account rimrocker like me, right? I'll tell ya this, bitch, you ain't good enough for me. I shoulda screwed you inside out the first night out, then killed ya. Well, this time, I'm making sure you die."

Jessie grunted, "You talk too much," and slapping Swann's gun aside, she bucked upward, bashing the top of her head into his face. Her gun hand came free, and she whipped him hard across the side of his face, throwing him on his back. As she came to her knees they both leveled their weapons, but Swann fired first. Jessie ducked and somersaulted backwards down the embankment, sliding helplessly toward the frigid churning waters. Swann fired at her, again too late, when he saw Ki running toward the bridge on foot.

Swann snatched up the saddlebag. In an animal crouch he dug his heels into the deep snow and charged uphill toward his broomtail, firing careless shots behind him and giving off an infernal roar. He threw himself into the saddle and lashed the horse into a downhill burst. Crossing the stream now was his only chance for escape. He descended through the cut as Ki made onto the bridge, gun drawn, and was startled by the body of Jessie's steeldust lying in his path. Desperately Swann

169

pulled his horse into a high-vaulting hurdle over the body. Ki held steadfastly to the middle of the bridge, holding his revolver with two hands and firing three shots into the animal's chest. Swann imagined he felt the impact. The bay's heart burst in mid-flight, and it had no legs when it hit the icy bridge. With a bone-shattering crash, the beast caromed sideways off the span, throwing its screaming rider headlong into the deathly cold flood and tearing a strip of lumber up from the structure with a ghastly screech and snap.

Ki leaped to the edge of the bridge and hung over to reach for Swann, but the bucking of the horse and the powerful current outdid him. Swann's screaming echoed through the gorge as he fought to stay above the icy flow sweeping him under the bridge. Ki jammed the pistol into his belt and lifted the shattered timber. With incredible effort he twisted it free and extended it over the downstream side. Kneeling, he waited for Swann to appear behind the horse's dead bulk.

Swann, as if empowered by an angry spirit belched from the foul mouth of hell itself, clung to the bridge beams beneath, cradling the stolen fortune over one arm. He screamed at the top of his lungs to fire his muscles as the life-stealing waters tugged at his legs and heavy clothing, urging him toward certain death. But Swann was the epitome of defiance. As Ki was tearing the splintered board from its last tenacious iron spikes Swann was lifting himself to the edge below Ki's feet. He had got the saddlebag and one elbow over the span when he felt his hip brush against a shelf of rock. He looked over. There was Ki, kneeling over the other side with his back to him, so Swann fished into the water and found a stone the size of a small cannon shot.

The sound of Swann struggling onto the bridge drew Ki around. He dropped the lumber at his feet. His hand moved for the pistol. The stone was already airborne and pounded Ki unexpectedly in the chest. He doubled up, expelling his last bit of breath, his fingers barely closed around the pistol grip. Swann loomed over him like a thunderhead and brutally kicked Ki's arm, flinging the gun into the snow across the bridge. With one hand Swann lifted his bruised enemy bodily and delivered a devastating blow to his face, that felt like a brace of horseshoes. Ki's body went limp, but Swann prevented him from falling. Another iron fist to his stomach nearly had Ki puking blood into the river as his ponytailed head dangled over the edge.

Swann lunged to find the buried pistol, but Ki scissored his legs, clipping Swann's at the ankles, and brought him down on his face. With snakelike agility Swann turned and booted Ki squarely in the jaw, numbing him and blurring his sight. He got to his feet and closed in for another attack. Ki nimbly sprung out of reach and stood between Swann and the saddle-bag, assuming the "saddle" stance of the martial artist, hands raised and open. Swann stood before him, exhaling vapor like a dragon.

Sizing him up, Ki was amazed Swann was still standing. His clothing was soaked in icy water. He had been grazed by bullets, tumbled from the saddle, nearly drowned, and still he came on with a supernatural fire in his eyes, the hint of a deranged grin, and an anger that would destroy everything in his path were he allowed to go on unchecked. His bare head was abominable, the thick, wrinkled scar seeming paler and waxier than Ki had imagined it. The scar ran deep in C. J. Swann, and Ki puzzled over where he found his limitless energy.

Ki readied himself, as if to face a charging bull. He concentrated on calming his own breath, refueling himself, suppressing the pain that pulsated throughout his chest. He rooted himself to the center of the earth.

"You're coming with us, Swann."

Swann scoffed. "In a pine box, pretty boy."

He closed in with a pile-driving jab, and Ki responded with a combined forearm block and a well-placed *choku-zuki,* a short forward punch, contacting Swann's rock-hard stomach. The impact would have dropped most other men. Instead, Ki thought he saw Swann smile as he dropped back. A lightning-fast forward snap kick to Swann's abdomen sent him back a step, but the scar-headed man advanced once more, like a man possessed. Ki delivered a flurry of iron-knuckled punches that didn't stun him, until Swann caught one in his palm and twisted it down, bringing Ki to one knee.

"You can't touch me, worm," Swann sniveled. "You don't know whose stream you're muddyin'."

"I know you're the ugliest goddamn cauliflower I ever saw on two shoulders, friend. I hear the squaw who cut you got all the brain you had. That's why you're stupid enough to think you're getting away."

Enraged, Swann drove his heavy fist into Ki's bruised ribs once, then again. He stood back and kicked the fallen warrior in the head, then ran for the bonds. Ki tried to trip him but missed. Swann seized the length of torn lumber. Wielding its splintered end like a spear, he lunged. Ki spun on his rump and kicked the shaft aside. Swann lifted it and hatcheted downward, but Ki rolled from under it easily and sprung to his feet. He could barely straighten up, his ribs were so bruised. He wasn't sure he could fight much longer. Drawing the lumber back like a club, Swann readied his final attack.

"Ki!" shouted Jessie.

The glint of slate-gray metal in midair. The weight of iron in his palm. He fumbled. The barrel . . . the hammer. . . . He looked at the peachwood grips and cried out, "Here!" and threw the Colt back to her.

Swann snorted, "Asshole," and swung.

With a circular forearm block with his opposite arm, Ki deflected the board upward and crouched. He hammered a cannonball fist into Swann's ribs and drove the heel of his other hand upward into his jaw, driving his teeth through his tongue. He spun around, bringing one leg up in an abrupt circular kick that left a heel scuff across Swann's ear and dazed him. Ki circled further, crushing Swann's exposed neck with a precisely delivered *empi-uchi,* the brutal elbow strike he had perfected long ago.

Still Swann hadn't let go of the lumber. To Ki's utter amazement the relentless outlaw thrust the end of the board into Ki's stomach, then again into his down-turned face. He dropped the wood, drew back a mighty fist, and pummeled Ki with enough power to send him back with his feet in the air. Swann bolted for the saddlebag, desperately trying to keep his footing on the slippery boards. He rushed past Ki and, sliding to a stop, ran his hands through the snow, looking for Ki's buried gun.

Groggily, Ki shook his head as he sat up. Swann's hands fanned through the fluffy whiteness frantically as Ki reached for the lacquered sheath in his waist-band. He found the handle of his *tanto*, flipped it into the air just inches from his face. Swann pulled the revolver from the snow. Ki caught the *tanto* by the tip of its curved blade and drew it back. Swann raised the weapon. The hammer lifted. Ki snapped the knife into a flicker and rolled. After precisely two turns, end over end, the blade pierced at the same instant the gun exploded. Swann's throat was pierced from front to back, while the bullet flattened itself in the old wood of the bridge, sizzling as it cooled beneath the melting snow.

Swann collapsed at the edge of the bridge, clutching his throat. The saddlebag left his hand, flaps open, and spilled its contents over the side. Thousands of dollars in bonds fluttered to the gushing white water below and rushed to follow the dead horse downstream. Gurgling with rage, drowning in his own blood, Swann frantically snatched for his vanishing fortune, clutching at the air, unable to reach the water or to stop the bonds from slipping out of the upturned bag. He yelled and cursed unintelligibly. Whether due to the cold or to his loss, his eyes teared, and when he succeeded in lifting the saddlebag and seeing it was empty, he quietly turned the pistol on Ki once more.

Choked with blood, his words, "You die with me," went unheard, drowned out by Jessie's cry, "Ki! Look out!" and the final explosive report of her Colt. And by the time the echo throughout the once-peaceful gorge died out, so had Charles Joseph Swann, his life spilling out the ragged exit wound in his forehead and disappearing into the rushing white water below.

★

Epilogue

Although senile old Winter finally recalled how mild the days should be in Sarah, Texas, some folks nonetheless were chilled to the core on the day they buried Deputy Marshal Boyd Barefoot amid the cottonwoods in the white-fenced churchyard. It had dawned a rainy day, but as the procession got under way, the skies opened and brightened just long enough for the reverend to deliver his eulogy and read from his gold-edged Bible, and for those interested to drop clods of earth upon the long box below. Then the clouds closed again, like the curtains on a stage, and began to shed their rainy tears. Some said a ray of light had swept right across those hallowed grounds, if not over the grave site itself. It was a day they talked about in Sarah for a long time thereafter.

Not many folks knew Barefoot a whit, but there were plenty on hand to honor his memory. Marshal Isaiah Haskins was one of them. Just returned from settling that nuisance tiff over grazing rights up north, he had been looking forward to spending time with his old friend Barefoot, get reacquainted. It was tragically ironic that Barefoot's strong medicine should be broken by a coward who wasn't even gunning for him; but then, Haskins figured, that's the way it should be. Accidents happen. No glory for cowards.

Jessie cried at Barefoot's grave, cried more than she had at the doleful double funeral for the Judd boys, a few days back, or for her own ranch hands before that. There was no way to separate the soulful connection she had with Barefoot from the physical one, and she was connected to him as no one else in Sarah was. She strove to remember him as he was when he was smiling, not how he died. The fear that she would forget how his voice sounded tormented her, and though she was certain his voice would come back to her, it was difficult to imagine it just then, as the loose handful of dirt slipped through her fingers like time, like life. Surely this had been an aging season.

Haskins invited Jessie and Ki to the Estevanico's Palmwood Room afterward, having no way of knowing what the place meant to Jessie. They were seated by a window apart from the few other patrons present. Outside stood an old, drooping willow, haggard and dripping in the rain. The room looked somehow different without Barefoot's presence.

"I got my tail back here quick as I could after Brant Adams telegraphed the newspaper up there," Haskins explained. "If only I'da got away sooner, I mighta had a chance to see Barefoot before all this. Missed y'all by just a few hours."

Ki mused, "If one thing could be different, everything could be different."

Haskin's pursed his lips while he fingered the silverware. "True enough."

Jessie said, "I couldn't believe it when I saw you and your men coming through the sage, Marshal."

Jokingly, Haskins replied, "Well, as town marshal investigating a crime, I think I've just been insulted."

"You know what I mean," Jessie said.

" 'Course I do, Miss Starbuck. And it's right fortunate I came when I did. I been scouting them hills for longer than I'd like to admit, ever since that Swann feller hitched his pony to Vargas' rail, and I never did flush him outta there. I ain't the tracker ol' Barefoot was, I guess, but the point is this: that boy I found lying up there in that cabin is gonna be all right, and with a little convincin' on my part, he's gonna testify and make a right smart case against Vargas."

"He agreed to that?" asked Jessie.

"Well, he was rebellious all right, but it was either that or face down a charge of attempted murder. Like that Dupree boy—I just sat down with him at the infirmary and told him what I intended on doing. He was facin' conspiracy to kidnap, murder, mayhem, horse theft. . . . Hell, I'm half ready to string him up myself. Now, he's foamin' at the mouth to redeem his own self."

"So what are the charges against Vargas?" Ki asked.

"That's the best part of all," Haskins sang, shifting in his seat.

The proprietor's daughter greeted them politely and set down a tray of fresh breads and pastries and refilled their cups with rich, black coffee. She left saying few words, knowing they were principal players in the recent tragic events.

"Conspiracy to kidnap, conspiracy to murder . . . they're just to start and all fairly simple with the testimony we got. That Dupree boy admitted them poker I.O.U.s were his—the ones Whittaker found in Barefoot's room. It's all in the deposition, but that's something good. Soon as I got into town and heard the whole story, I deputized some o' the boys and sent 'em out to fetch Vargas, and guess what? In a safe, in his big ol' private office, they found a handsome little Remington-Elliot Derringer—mother-of-pearl grips, nice engraving, .32, and his father's initials on it to boot. Packs a wallop, and easy to conceal, too." Jessie hooted with joy as Haskins dunked a pastry in his coffee and continued, "Don Wilfredo says the gun is his, but . . ."

He swung his jaw and wrapped his face around the large, sopping sweetdough.

"And Leslie Sykes?" Ki inquired.

Haskins answered with his mouth full. "I'm obliged to make sure the murder charge sticks, no matter how much we all would have liked to pull that trigger our own selves. Ol' Vargas might have killed her father, and I'll bet he did, but provin' it's a different thing. Besides, two wrongs don't make a right, and I told her so."

With a knowing smile, Ki said, "What did she say to that?"

The marshal laughed. " 'It sure felt right to me,' she said! She's a hellion, that one. . . . As far as all that gibber-jabber about land fraud and deeds, the Spanish crown and what not, I don't know much about that, but to my ears, it sounds like the lady's got something. But I'll let her tell you all about that her own self, because I'm offering to make a small concession. That's what I really wanted to talk to y'all about.

"Now I don't see as how Miss Sykes is gonna be any danger to no one else; she already did what she intended on doing—assuming that she planned to kill old man Vargas—that's for the jury to decide. So I was intending on letting her wait out the hearing outside o' that smelly old cell. I was inclined to ask you, Miss Starbuck, to look after her, but being as y'all are a witness in her case, that might muddy up the stream some. So, if you're agreeable to it, Master Ki, I'm proposing to release her in your recognizance, pending the hearing. Don't make no sense keeping the lady in the hoosegow if she ain't gonna run from something she ain't ashamed of. And as far as I can see, that girl ain't ashamed o' nothin'! "

Caught off guard, Ki was flustered with surprise. "What do I have to do?"

"Put your fingers inside me."

Ki moaned in affirmation. He drew Leslie Sykes' legs farther apart, and keeping his mouth against her delicious vulva, he spread the soft inner lips and slipped two fingers into her sopping wet vagina, sending warm spasms of delight up her spine. She responded by gripping his thickly engorged member more firmly, yanking and twisting it, sucking on it more feverishly. Ki's pelvis swayed involuntarily, thrusting deeper into her hungry, squealing, slurping mouth.

They lay on their sides, head-to-hip, like the double interlocking swirl of the yin and yang that was the symbol of the Lone Star duo. It was no more than three hours since Miss Sykes had been released in Ki's charge, and they had already spent nearly an hour entangled in each other's embraces. She had insisted on taking a room at the Estevanico, where a hot bath and gourmet meal were her first priorities. Ki, of course, had delivered her few belongings to her room, at which time Miss Sykes made it very clear that he was her second, more important, priority. This was just as Ki had hoped, and he made himself fully available to her sensual pursuit, taking his every cue from her advances. They were opposites—except where passion was concerned. Her initiative dovetailed with his responsiveness. His fiery intensity and her watery persistence fused in a sexuality so honest and direct that to have stayed apart would not only have been impossible, but also unnatural.

Every time they had brushed shoulders on the stairway or her fingers had lingered upon his as he handed her bags to her, the embers of desire within them were kindled until blazing. Their conversation about Leslie's dilemma had dwindled in importance with each initial kiss. And when Ki's tongue first traced a cool line up her slender neck and behind her ear, all talk turned simple, if not primitive. They bared themselves with little ceremony and danced the ancient dance that has little room for words.

Useless for talk, Ki's tongue now circled and pressed the enlarged pearl of her clitoris as his fingers massaged her smooth, pink interior. His face was damp with her sex, and his eyes, half-closed with hypnotic pleasure, devoured the sight of this most pleasant of valleys. His thumbs dimpled the plush hillocks of her ass. His chin explored the dense thickets of her pubis. His hands tickled and teased the pucker lying at the valley floor on their erotic excursions toward her spine. His determined fingers plumbed her most secret depths.

Her slender, white legs spread like wings, admitting Ki to the central core of her being. Her legs began to quiver with erotic anticipation as the muscles of her abdomen tightened and that irresistible tickle in her vulva accumulated. Her toes flared in midair, mindless, tense, electric. She held the tip of his rock-hard shaft in her mouth as her hand pumped fast and hard until she melted with her first saturating orgasm, leaving her spine livid and her chest shining in sweat.

Ki lifted himself to his knees. Keeping her legs spread wide, he straddled the lower one as she remained on her side and wrapped her upper leg around his waist. Guiding his slathered erection into her thick, black hair, he rubbed it between her labia, slid it across her opening, and drew a glistening trail of moisture all the way up the excited crease of her ass. He stretched her labia apart with it, teasing her and himself with brief forays inside her, then circled and pressed upon her engorged pearl until he could wait no longer.

He drove deep into her vagina, withdrew, and thrust again. The pleasure was all-consuming. He gripped her fleshy buttock in his large palm, and hooking the other arm around her thigh, he proceeded to pump his hips madly. Further aroused, she anchored her legs wherever she could, grabbed hold of Ki's knees, and bucked her pelvis wildly, driving her ruby clitoris against the hilt of Ki's sword every time he thrusted. He touched the joining of their bodies. He felt himself penetrating and stretching her delicate folds, and he spread her wider still, massaging her throbbing muscle between her two openings. She gasped. Moans and whimpering cries escaped her parted lips. Her eyes clenched with

180

sensual visions, and the pace of her thrusts increased.

Ki felt the unstoppable surge begin. His chest flushed, sweat erupted from every pore, he bled sweat and tasted sweat and rained sweat from his nose and forehead. His sexual soul descended through his body and gathered itself behind his cock and, in a huge locomotive heave, pulsed through him and into the gyrating woman. With a gut-searing groan, he forced himself as deep as he could go. Leslie's thrusts became a frenzy. She cried out in a long lifting moan. Her movements became jerky, and she followed Ki with a clenching orgasm that doubled her over and clamped her legs shut on Ki's beating member. He collapsed across her smooth, sculpted hip as the last contractions of Leslie's pussy squeezed him out with a tickle that made him flinch.

When they caught their breaths, they laughed and kissed. Feeling sleepy, Ki sat up on the sweat-and-cum-drenched bed. He sighed as he gathered his jet-black hair behind him. He tried to stand, but his knees mutinied and he fell back to bed.

"As prisoner," he huffed, "of the great state of Texas . . . in my charge . . . you are hereby ordered . . . to appear . . . for additional rehabilitation later this evening . . . and until further notice."

Leslie chuckled and gave his forearm a warm, tight squeeze.

Nearly one week later Jessie was preparing for her long-overdue return to the Circle Star Ranch as Ki looked on from a chair in the tidy room at Pritchard's. She hadn't seen as much of Ki as usual these past several days, but Jessie well understood the requirements of Ki's position. Early in the week Miss Sykes had successfully filed a devastating suit against Wilfredo Vargas and his operations, resulting in rapidly placed injunctions upon the bulk of his routine business, most of it related to tenant fees and right-of-way licenses. Attorneys across the state were aghast with news of the strength of her case. The affidavits Miss Sykes had brought back from Spain, bearing the seal of the Spanish crown, seemed incontrovertible and proved

Vargas' 1773 deed a fake. Suddenly new plaintiffs appeared, like moths to a flame, filing reclamation suits amounting to tens of thousands of dollars in damages, costs, and acreage. Railways, mines, cattlemen, drovers, coach lines, and a passel of smaller merchants, craftsmen, and traders lined up for their share of the spoils from the imminent Vargas cataclysm, following the lone, sharp-eyed woman whom they regarded as nothing less than a new Joan of Arc.

As Jessie gathered her newly washed shirts Ki said, "So even though she may never avenge her father's murder, it looks very likely that she'll topple Vargas."

"Sounds like David did Goliath," Jessie interjected.

"Might wipe him out completely after it's all said and done."

"Which may be a worse punishment for thieves like the Vargas family than one of them being hung for murder—although, given no other choice, I'd opt for that, all right."

She scooped some folded denims, piled them together with the shirts, and held the flap of her saddlebag open before packing them. Light entered the leather through a pair of bullet holes. Ki knew by her pause that she was reliving her close call on the bridge.

"You miss Boyd?" he asked softly.

Jessie blinked, about to speak. She closed the bag. Her lip trembled. With a deep breath she looked up bravely and said, "It hurts, Ki. Real bad."

Ki was silent, but his steady eyes were eloquent.

She said, "Just another heap of hurt to take with me, I guess. I ain't got enough already."

"It won't last."

She smirked and shook her head. "You don't really believe that, do you?"

Ki shook his head. She stuffed the bag and closed the flap. Finished. A thought crossed her mind that made a smile etch itself across her forlorn expression.

"Them bonds sure didn't last," she laughed. "They're about as gone as they could get. Here, Ki, help me with that one."

Ki hefted a satchel from the floor as Jessie threw the saddlebags over her shoulder.

"What will you do about them?" he asked.

She shrugged. "I telegraphed the broker. He said he could invalidate them and issue new ones. They'll be worthless if any one turns them in. Just pretty little pieces of paper, is all."

Outside, sunshine was returning to West Texas. It felt good on Jessie's face; took the chill out of the air almost as well as seeing a Circle Star buckboard and two of her better bronc peelers waiting for her. She greeted them as Ki handed the satchel over.

"Stay alert, fellas," he said, "and get her home quick. She needs her rest."

Jessie sighed, "I can't wait to fall into my own bed again. When will I see you?"

Ki replied, "Probably not before you return to testify."

"I'll miss you."

She gave him a hug and climbed into the wagon. Down the street, she noticed, Leslie Sykes stood outside the Estevanico wearing a veiled hat.

"So what do you think about Miss Sykes?" she asked.

Ki thought it over and said, "I think she's a very intelligent, very dignified, unrepentant minx."

"Unique," Jessie replied sullenly. "I hope she's no trouble. See you, Ki. And thanks."

Sadness in her voice. Ki knew it would take time for her to regain her vivacious buoyancy. She had lost it for now; but there had been losses on all sides. It was an aging season for all. And like all seasons, this was finally drawing to a close to advance the cycle. It was good for her to begin again at home.

Despite the magnificent landscapes changing hue beneath clouds scudding before the wind, the ride was anything but rewarding. Every mile between Sarah and the point where she had been kidnapped was fraught with vivid memories—the oddly flat sound of Leslie Sykes's pistol in the courtyard . . . the terrifying sight of Ki being shot . . . Tatum's brutal death . . .

183

Boyd's final expressions ... the lifeless white scar of that devil, Caddo Jack Swann. She looked west toward the broken, barren lands that concealed the snow-lined ridges beyond and swore she would put it all out of her mind, all the horrors of the mountain cabin. She wished no one would ever lay eyes on that haunted, pain-filled place again, unaware that if someone ever did, what they would find was one of Ki's own *shuriken*, with its metal ray embedded in the lintel of the door, a throwing star bearing the circled-S brand of the Starbuck family, standing as a reminder to some—and a warning to others.

If you enjoyed this book, subscribe now and get...

TWO FREE

A $7.00 VALUE—